NAKED BETRAYAL

The Conspiracy Murder

A Tony Felice, PI, Mystery

Geno Azevedo

NAKED BETRAYAL
The Conspiracy Murder

Copyright © 2014 by Geno Azevedo

A Tony Felice, PI, Mystery
www.TonyFeliceMystery.com

Design and layout by Mark E. Anderson
www.AquaZebra.com

Cover illustration by Ed Freeman Photography
www.edfreeman.com

Print on Demand by Lightning Source
A division of Ingram Books

Azevedo Publishing Company
Palm Springs, CA

Because of the dynamic nature of the Internet, any web addresses or links contained in this book may have changed since publication and may no longer be valid.

ISBN: 978-0-9904090-0-7

ISBN lists Azevedo Publishing Company as the publisher

Library of Congress Control Number: 2014908850

Printed in the United States of America

First Edition
First Printing, June 2014

Dedication

To my early mentor in life and good friend,
Benn Pasquini, for being such an integral
part in my development and guidance with finding
myself after my coming-out.

You have been like a big brother to me and
I looked up to you at that time of my life.

This one's for you, Benn -- Thanks.

Disclaimer

This book is a work of fiction. The characters, incidents, and dialogue are drawn from the author's imagination and are not to be construed as real. Any resemblance to actual events or persons, living or dead, is entirely coincidental.

About the Author

Geno is no stranger to the naturist community and he has chosen to share his life experiences vicariously with you thru the character of Antonio Vito Felice, PI. This is the third book in the series, the first being NAKED DICK and the second NAKED INNOCENCE.

He is a native Californian who worked for many years in Public Service employment before his retirement to Palm Springs. The desert sun provides ample opportunity to enjoy life with little or no textile confinement and writing is a good pastime.

Contents

NAKED BETRAYAL

The Conspiracy Murder

A Tony Felice, PI, Mystery

Geno Azevedo

Preface

The Conspiracy Murder

We were headed down the hall away from our cabin when suddenly we heard a loud scream followed by more screams and gasps.

"Now what?" I looked over at Brad and the two of us began to move swiftly in the direction of the main atrium lobby. Our floor was one of the mezzanine floors that overlooked the atrium. We looked down at the mass confusion on the floor below and still were not sure what the hysteria was about. There were several others now gathered, looking over the railing down onto the floor. I asked a guy next to us, *"Do you know what's going on? What's all the hysteria about?"*

"I want to get closer and see if I can identify the body." The Private Investigator in me was coming out. I was curious. From where we were I could only tell that it appeared to be a young man of slight frame.

1

Vacation Planning

It was a typical spring morning in San Diego with a slight chill in the air from the bit of overcast that had rolled in from the ocean overnight. The fog would soon burn off and be totally gone by noon leaving a warm, sunny day -- much too nice to be sitting at my desk working. If it were a weekend, I'd be headed for Black's Beach to strip down and soak up some sun on my now pale body, the effects of a long cool winter. But this was Monday and I had a lot of paperwork to get caught up on at my office.

Having recently wrapped up my investigation on a rather involved murder case, I needed to be sure all the details were documented in the case file and the police report was available for viewing before I filed this one away.

My boss here at Balboa Private Investigators is a stickler on details. However, Vinnie is more than just a boss to me -- he's been a good friend too. I've worked for Vince Castillo for several years now but my goal in life is to make a name for myself and establish my own investigation agency.

Our agency investigates anything and everything, and it was after a suspected murder case four years ago that my cohorts here started calling me the Naked Dick.

It was actually my first case going out into the field undercover as an investigator. The unique situation of this case allowed Vinnie to give me my big break – he needed a guy to infiltrate a gay nudist camp in Sacramento. And yes I am gay, but I was certainly not a nudist at that time, so my undercover skills were really put to the test.

I like to brag that I did crack the case and discovered indeed there had been a murder that had taken place and not just an accidental drowning. Along the way on that adventure, I made some lasting friendships with guys that I still keep in touch with. I discovered I enjoyed a life free of textiles and the people I meet are so sincere. Not having designer labels or fashion sense to rely on, they manage to influence people only with their personality …and in some cases a little "eye candy" as well. And now I spend much of my free time at Black's Beach au naturel.

The case I just wrapped up took place right here in San Diego. I was asked to investigate the death of a dear friend. This was a difficult one for me since I was so close to the victim. As it turned out I ended up solving not only that case, but along the way solved another crime in conjunction with his murder. In the process of my investigation, I nearly got myself killed -- but that's all part of the job. It all worked out for the best, and I walked away from that case with a huge payoff. Of course I would rather still have my friend with us, but I'm adjusting to the loss.

Buzz ...buzz. My desk phone startled me as I sat day dreaming. "Yes, Jenn ...good morning!"

"Good morning, Tony. I have a call for you. It's Robb with ExtaSea Cruises."

"Oh great! Thanks, Jenn, put him through."

After such a sizable bonus from my last investigation, I told my partner, Brad, I'd take him on an extravagant cruise vacation to celebrate our two year anniversary of our committed relationship and living together. We've been in the planning stages of this cruise for about a month now so hopefully our friend and travel agent, Robb, has been able to pin down a really kewl trip for us.

At work I try to be as professional as possible, even with people I know. "Good morning, this is Tony Felice speaking. How may I help you?"

"Morning, Tony. It's Robb. I hope you had a good weekend. I've been working on locating a nice cruise itinerary for you two and I think I might have something."

"Great, Robb, let's hear it."

"I know you said you weren't all that concerned that

this be a gay or straight cruise -- you just wanted it to be an awesome vacation."

"Yep, that's what I'm looking for. Brad and I want to make some memories together and do some traveling."

"Well, I think I have the best of both worlds for you."

"Don't keep me in suspense!"

"I just learned this morning that V.I.P. Gay Cruise Vacations has commissioned the *Serendipity of the Seas* for a repositioning cruise, taking passengers in the process of relocating from the west coast to the east, thru the Panama Canal. I should be receiving some brochures on this cruise in the next day or so and will send out some information to you when I do."

"Wow! That sounds really kewl. I've always wanted to take that trip some day."

"Yes, it sounds great. You would cut through the locks in the Panama Canal which in itself is an adventure. The cruise leaves right here from San Diego and ends up in Miami. It's a ten day cruise. I still don't have all the ports of call for you yet, but I'm working on that."

"Sounds wonderful, Robb. What are the dates for this?"

"It leaves San Diego on the 14th of September. I think you told me you wanted to plan something for the end of the year but before the weather changes. I think this is an ideal time."

"Sounds like it to me too. Not sure about Brad's schedule with the start of school, but we can work it out,

I'm sure. Thanks."

"As I said, I'll send more information this week for you and Brad to look over and if you decide you want to do this, let me know right away. This one is going to book up fast. I'd need a twenty percent deposit from you to reserve a cabin."

"Thanks. I'm sure once the word gets out in the gay community, this cruise will be popular. We'll make up our minds and get back to you, Robb. Thanks again."

"Sure thing, Tony. Don't wait too long though. Watch your mail this week. I'll get information to you soon. Thanks for your business, Tony."

"Thank you, Robb. I'll be in touch soon. Take care."

"You too, Tony, and tell Brad hello for me. ...Bye."

"Will do and thanks again."

I'd been on a few cruises in the past, but never an all gay cruise and I've always wanted to take that trek through the locks of the Canal. As far as I know, Brad has never taken a cruise before. We've only been living together in a committed relationship for about two years now, so I'm still discovering things about this man.

We'd dated some time ago but had a very unfortunate break up. We've both grown up a lot since then. At that time Brad was not ready to settle down to one steady relationship and he hurt me badly when I caught him cheating on me after thinking we were a monogamous couple. Then after several years with no contact, and time for each of us to mature somewhat, we re-connected. We began to date once again and the rest is history. We have a really fulfilling, close relationship now and communicate well with each other. I'm at a good stage of my life and enjoy having Brad to share it with me.

As I sat there at my desk thinking of Brad and our vacation, my iPhone rang -- the all too familiar piano riff ring tone assigned to Brad -- and his face lit up the screen.

"Morning, Brad. ...Actually, it's almost afternoon, isn't it?"

"Morning, Hon. I'm just taking a break here from grading finals. I'm about to go cross eyed. How has your Monday morning gone?" Brad is a Psychology Professor at the University and recently earned his doctorate degree. Doctor Brad Fisher sounds so important but to me he is my Babe.

"It's gone well, Babe. I just got off the phone with Robb with information about our cruise plans."

"Great! Good news, I hope?"

"Yes, very, I think. He found us an all gay cruise on a ship that's repositioning to the east coast. I can talk with you more about the details this evening when you get home."

"Look forward to that. I might be home late. Trying to wrap things up here and getting the grades registered in the computer for notices to go out."

"Not a problem, Babe. I'll fix something for dinner

that will keep well and we can eat when you get home."

"Thanks. See you this evening, Tony. I'd better get back at it here."

"Okay. See you whenever you get home. Love you ...bye."

We live in a fairly new fifth-floor condo in the Hillcrest area of San Diego. I love living in this little enclave with all the quaint shops and restaurants, all within walking distance. Some of the best times spent with Brad have been just sipping wine on the balcony and watching the sun set on the ocean in the distance. We keep a lap blanket on the love seat just for such occasions. It never takes me long to snuggle up next to Brad under that blanket. Any time I can spend wrapped up in his arms makes me feel safe and secure.

Buzz ... buzz. Here I was day dreaming again. It was difficult to concentrate on work, knowing it was such a beautiful day outside.

"Yes, Jenn."

"Tony, Mr. Castillo just came in and he asked me to have you step into his office."

"Okay. Thanks, Jenn. I'll be right there."

Now, what could he possibly want this morning? It's not often that Vinnie calls any of his agents into his office to talk and we're always leery when he does. Oftentimes, though, we end up getting assigned to an unusual and interesting case. I grabbed a note pad and headed down the hall to Vinnie's office.

I poked my head inside. "Excuse me, Vinnie, you wanted to see me?"

"Yes, yes, Tony. Good morning, come in, come in. ... Have a seat."

"Thanks."

Vinnie's voice softened and he cleared his throat before he spoke. "Tony, I'm sure you realize how proud I am of you and the skill you've shown at this office as an investigator over the past eight years. You've really represented this agency and me as the owner very well."

I could feel myself starting to blush from his praises but it was good to hear that my commitment to the agency was appreciated. "Thank you, Vinnie, that's always nice to hear. It's actually been ten years that I've been here now. "

"Well, damn it, you deserve the recognition. And, because of that, I wanted to talk to you about a little proposition I have for you."

He really had me curious now.

"Tony, for many years, long before you started working here for me, I've dealt with a heart condition. I never told anyone about it, except of course my wife knows."

"Gosh, I'm sorry to hear that." My upbeat demeanor suddenly changed. I felt sadness for him.

"Well, that's how it goes, Tony. You have to play the hand you're dealt, right?"

"I guess."

Vinnie seemed to be more relaxed having gotten that confession off his chest and he leaned back in his office chair to continue. "It's come to the point with me that my doctor feels I should retire or at least not be working as much as I am. He says it's not doing me any good. Although I think sometimes he doesn't know what he's talking about."

I chuckled to myself at that comment as it reminded me of my own father.

"There's no way that I'm ready to sell the agency -- not at this point anyway. But I realize I do need to move further away from the business end of things."

"Well, if there's anything I can do to lighten your load here and keep the operation flowing smoothly, let me know. You've managed to build up quite an excellent reputation."

Vinnie leaned forward, elbows on his desk. "Thanks, Tony, but that's all because of you and my other investigators. And that's why I'd like to ask you to take over the operations of this office and be my CEO. That would allow me to stay out of the way and let you run the day-to-day business."

"Maybe someday," he added, "I can even sell the business to you, Tony."

My eyes widened. "Wow, I don't know what to say. This is so sudden, and I'm very moved by your offer. Being your CEO is something I'd really like, Vinnie, but I'd appreciate a few days to consider it." I was totally shocked with his proposition and I'm sure my face showed it.

"Certainly. You deserve it, Tony, and you realize of course you would be getting a sizable salary increase. However, the downside is that you probably won't be working as many investigation cases and will be spending more time in the office."

"Sure, I understand, Vinnie. I can tell you now that I am very interested in your offer but I want to run it by Brad as well."

"Not a problem, Tony. Let me put together a contract proposal so you can compare the salary and job description and what I would expect from you. Then if you could let me know in, say …two weeks from now?"

I was still in shock and could hardly speak. "No problem, Vinnie. I can let you know before that, I'm sure."

"Great. I really hope you'll accept this proposal as I don't want to go outside the agency to recruit and I don't feel that confident with any of my other agents here. I just don't feel they have what it takes to keep a business like this running smoothly. All my agents are good in the field with investigating, but as you seem to know there's a lot more to the nuts and bolts of this operation. And what you don't know, I've no doubt you can pick up readily.

"I'll have Jenn prepare that contract proposal and get it to you by mid week. Then we can discuss it further if you like and you can let me know what you think.

Thanks, Tony …for all that you do."

"Thank you, Vinnie." I stood up and shook his hand and hoped that my legs would carry me as I walked out of his office. I managed to make it back to my office before allowing myself to grin from ear to ear with excitement. What an amazing roll of the dice in my favor. My life is good.

2

New Horizons

The rest of my day at the office after my meeting with Vinnie was a blur and for the drive home I was on auto pilot. I had so much I wanted to tell Brad I didn't know where to start. Since Brad had told me he'd be a little late getting home, I knew I had some time to relax with a glass of wine and try to reflect on all that was going on in my life.

Stepping off the elevator and walking down the hall to the front door of our condo, I couldn't help but recall the evening that Brad and I reconnected for our first date after having been apart for so long.

That evening, seeing him approach me as I watched and waited in the hall, I was totally aroused by this sexy man. He was sporting a black Dolce & Gabbana v-neck cashmere pullover that flattered his hairy chest and gave him a masculine, rugged appearance. With his sleeves pushed up and his hairy forearms exposed, and the bold Movado watch on his wrist that complemented his tan skin, he rocked that look and it still turns me on. I've always been attracted to hairy chests and arms on a man. Brad is slightly taller than I am, so we fit nicely together as a couple. His thick hair of light brown, wavy and worn full but meticulously manicured, his dreamy blue eyes, accentuated with the tint on his contact lenses, and his moderately hairy body is the full package, all of which I find quite sexy, and I am very fortunate to have him in my life.

As I sat on the burgundy leather couch with the brushed chrome frame and looked around at our home, a feeling of accomplishment came over me. The cool blue-gray painted walls complement the blond hardwood floor and both offer a feeling of peace and serenity. Fortunately, Brad and I are both pretty much neat freaks and so our place is always a comfortable, elegant place free of clutter.

As I began to relax and focus on the conversation with my boss earlier in the day, I couldn't help but smile. I felt so blessed. There was little doubt that I wanted to accept Vinnie's generous offer, but I still needed to give serious consideration to the pros and cons of being the office CEO. I'd surely not have as much field work any longer and I might miss that part of my job. And the bonuses would be pretty much a thing of the past, although the higher salary should make up for that. Also, I felt this was something I needed to discuss with

Brad as our relationship is based on sharing with one another. I value Brad's opinion and he might be able to offer me advice and unbiased input as someone not directly involved with the decision.

I was on my second glass of wine when I heard the keys in the door. Brad was home …all was good.

"So, Hon, what's all this news you had to tell me?" We were sitting at Wang's in North Park where I'd made last-minute dinner reservations. Seated on the mezzanine level at our favorite banquette overlooking the dining room below, I was glad I'd decided to come to Wang's so we could relax and just talk, rather than fuss over cooking and cleaning up. Besides, it's one of our favorite dining spots in San Diego and any excuse to go there works for the both of us.

"I don't know where to start. I guess with the cruise probably." I was feeling like a kid with a secret just busting inside to tell. "You know I talked to Robb today and he has what sounds like a super cruise in mind for us. He's going to be sending us some brochures to look over later and decide. And …if we want to go, we need to act fast as this is a repositioning cruise and it will likely fill up fast."

Brad looked somewhat puzzled. "So what exactly is a

repositioning cruise? What does that mean?"

"It's a one-time only, one-way, ten day cruise from the west coast to the east."

"Okay, I have heard of that. So the ship will then be permanently docked on the east coast, at least for the season?"

"Exactly."

Brad was now beaming with excitement at the thought. "It sounds amazing, Tony, from what you said earlier and I like the fact that it's an all gay cruise and that it's going through the Canal. I've never been on a cruise before let alone going through the locks and channels of the Panama Canal for my first one."

"Yeah, I was wondering if this was your first cruise. And I like the all gay cruise thing too. I'll bet we'll know other guys on the trip. Remember those two guys we met in Palm Springs the time we went to the Gentlemen's Martini Night at Spencer's Racquet Club restaurant? They'd been on something like -- sixteen cruises and go on at least two a year? Maybe they'll be going."

"I don't recall that ...you sure I was part of that conversation?" Brad had a look on his face like he was searching to recall this incident meeting these two guys.

"You were there. Remember, we really liked the two of them. One of the guys had a concierge business in Palm Springs and the other was retired from the airlines. I know the one guy is John but I don't recall his partner's name."

"Oh yeah, now I remember …John and Craig. Nice guys. That would be fun to see them again. Wish we knew how to get in touch with them."

"Well, with as many cruises as they go on, I wouldn't be surprised if they're going."

We'd finished our cosmos just in time for the arrival of our dinner. We love the dim sum at Wang's but tonight we'd gone for a variety dinner for two with the honey walnut shrimp and the drunken chicken won ton appetizers.

"So when the brochures arrive for the cruise we can look them over and decide. I look forward to going with you on your first cruise experience, a cruise virgin, and this one sounds perfect.

"Now, let me tell you my other good news!" I could hardly contain myself any longer.

"I can tell you're just dying to tell me something. So what is it you're so excited about?"

"I am …excited, that is, to tell you. So today at work, Vinnie …you know Vinnie, my boss?"

"Yeah, of course I know Vinnie," Brad assured me.

"Well, Vinnie called me into his office, and you know we never know what to expect when he wants to talk to any of us. Needless to say I was very curious. …So turns out …Vinnie wants to cut back on managing the office and he wants me to be his CEO."

Brad's eyes opened wide. "Oh my God, Hon, that's wonderful. How exciting for you!"

"You have no idea. ...He has some health issues and said if he ever decides to sell the agency, he'd seriously consider selling to me! Brad, this is something I've been working towards for years. I've always wanted to run my own agency. And as sad as the circumstances are, I'm sure eventually Vinnie will have to sell the business."

"And I'm guessing as the CEO you'll be making a lot more money as well?" Brad sounded more like a proud father now, beaming with pride.

"Yes, but at this point I still need to see the contract proposal. I'll make more money but will have less time in the field because it'll be mostly an office job. That's the trade-off. One good part is that being the CEO, I'll be able to have flexibility with my hours."

"That is such great news, Tony. I'm so happy for you."

"So you think I should do it?"

"Hell yeah, as long as the contract looks good to you ...go for it!"

That was reassuring to me. "Thanks, Babe. So glad to hear you say that." We raised our wine glasses to toast my promotion.

We finished our dinner over more small talk and headed back home. It was destined to be a romantic evening for us after all the joy and good news we'd shared.

We poured another glass of wine and after stripping down to our boxer shorts, stepped out onto the balcony to enjoy the cool evening air. This was one of my favorite times with Brad, cuddled in his arms under a blanket on the love seat. We'd repeated this scene many times before but tonight seemed special to me. I'd so much to be thankful for.

The slight buzz I felt from the wine and the warmth of Brad's body next to mine were getting to me. I ran my hand over his muscled, hairy chest and felt that familiar, erotic tingle in my crotch as my cock began to stiffen. He leaned down to kiss me, but not a traditional kiss. He began to tease me with his tongue and little bites to my lips. He had me totally aroused and in no time at all, the tingle had become a full-on erection. With his arms wrapped around me, I could feel his dick pressing against my back side and the passion between us intensifying. We decided to move inside to the bedroom and continue with our obsession.

The once restrictive underwear spotted with pre cum now lay in a bunch on the floor beside the bed. With Brad's naked sexy image before me in the dimly lit bedroom, his cock now fully engorged, I couldn't take my gaze off him. Our mouths continued intensely kissing and our tongues writhed together. I could feel the slight stubble of his day old beard on his cheeks. That was a turn-on for me. His hairy masculine chest and those strong legs that I've had wrapped around me many times during his climax, brought to mind nights of passionate love making. I love that feeling of his muscles tensed and building up for the eruption of his dick inside me. I wanted so bad now to have him on top of me and to feel him thrusting his pelvis to my buttocks, over and over again. I began squirming at the thought. He was all too familiar with this ritual we had and was more than happy to fulfill my desires. We continued with passionate kissing and fondling and before I knew it, we had both climaxed.

Our sweaty bodies now resting …our breathing now beginning to calm, I could feel the sticky cum from my own ejaculation on my chest and the thought of knowing that we were so sexually compatible was euphoric for me. We both fell fast asleep in a spoon position. Brad was beside me …all was good.

∾

"Morning, Jenn. Where does the weekend go?" It was Monday morning and I was back at work, knowing that I'd be making a decision this week that would affect the rest of my life.

"Oh hi …good morning, Tony." Jenn seemed a little stressed already this morning and it was only nine o'clock. "Mr. Castillo asked me to come in early this morning and prepare something for you so that it would be ready when you came in. I'm just finishing up and I'll bring it right in to you."

"Thanks, Jenn. Don't rush."

Jenn smiled at me and gave me a thumbs-up mouthing a whisper of congratulations.

Within ten minutes, Jenn delivered the contract proposal for the CEO position that Vinnie had offered me. I spent most of the morning reading it over and over and I couldn't find anything about it that was negative. The salary increase was most generous in spite of losing investigative bonuses, and the flexibility of my time still seemed to be a desirable part of the job.

This was a step towards the future for me to someday run my own business. I felt for certain that, after all the time and money that Vinnie had invested into this agency over the years, when he did decide to sell, he'd be very selective about whom he sold to. I felt this new job would put me in a good position to be his first choice when the time came.

Buzz ...buzz! My desk phone broke my concentration and the speculations about my future.

"Yes, Jenn?"

"Tony, I have someone on the phone for you, but ah ...I'm not sure what he said his name is. I asked him twice and it sounded like Ben Eade or Bun ney? Sorry!"

3

Bon Voyage

I knew who was calling right away when I heard "Bunny." His real name is Blaine, from Portland -- the young, flamboyant, aspiring artist that I'd befriended on a plane ride to Sacramento a couple of years ago. That was during my undercover assignment at a nudists resort to investigate a murder. And it was before I realized that I enjoyed the nudist lifestyle and the freedom from textiles. Blaine was a large part of that life-changing discovery for me.

"Good morning, this is Tony Felice. How may I help you?" Just in case my instincts were wrong, I thought I'd better sound professional.

"Hey, you sexy thang, how's life treating you?"

I could recognize that bubbly, vibrant voice anywhere. It was Blaine. "Hey, Bunny, how are you? ... What a surprise."

"I'm great, Babes ...and how have you been, Mr. PI Man?"

He made me smile. "Really good, Blaine. Just considering a big promotion here with the agency and my love life is wonderful."

"Wow, that's good news. ...I've got some good news too!" Blaine sounded excited. "I'm going to be your new neighbor. I'm moving to San Diego to try and get some more of my paintings sold and get my name out there."

"Great, Blaine. I think you should do well with the affluent people in San Diego. I've got someone here I want to introduce you to. He's a retired famous movie director, loves art and is very wealthy. You might recognize the name, Robert de Saint Cyr."

"Yeah, that sounds like a good combination and someone I want to meet ...wealthy and famous, loves art. The name does sound familiar."

"I'm happy for you, Blaine. ...So when are you going to be in town here again? It would be great to get together. I'm anxious for you to meet Brad too."

"I should be there in a couple of weeks and all moved by the end of summer so I can still enjoy some nice weekends at Black's Beach.

"Well, Tony, I should let you get back to work, but I was just thinking about you and wanted to let you know the good news. And ...congratulations on your promotion too."

"Thanks for calling, Blaine. Good talking to you and keep in touch so we can get together next time you're in town. We'll have to plan a beach day when you get settled here."

∽

That week went by very fast for me, meeting with Vinnie to learn some of the responsibilities of my new job. I realized how much about the agency and the business end of things that I didn't know. Nothing I couldn't learn or handle over time.

The cruise brochures from Robb arrived that week also and Brad and I had a major decision to make -- deciding if we were serious about going on this cruise. It all sounded so wonderful, a vacation to remember.

Getting ready for work Friday morning I reminded Brad while he was in the shower, "Babe, don't forget we have lunch plans today. I'll meet you along with Robb at Bronx Pizza in the Hillcrest to discuss the cruise details."

"Yes, Hon, I have it in my Outlook and I won't forget. We're going to do this, right?"

"I'm looking forward to it. I'll probably need a vacation after a few months working this new job." I had to chuckle at the thought.

We met with Robb from ExtaSea Cruises and booked the V.I.P. all gay cruise. We couldn't wait to board the *Serendipity* for an adventure through the locks of the Panama Canal and make some vacation memories together.

The summer went by really fast, it seemed, and here we were in September packing for the cruise. I had managed to move effortlessly into my new career in management and I had the office running smoothly. I always knew if given the chance, I would be a good manager. Having come up through the ranks and starting at the bottom, I had compassion for my staff and so I was respected by them and well liked. With the confidence I have in my office staff, I felt I could leave for vacation and with good conscience, knowing everything would run well in my absence.

Thankfully the ship departed from the pier right in San Diego which was nice. Coming home, of course, we would be flying back from Miami.

"Babe, do you think you should try on your tux? We haven't worn them since the party aboard Robert de Saint Cyr's yacht."

With a bit of sarcasm, Brad responded, "I don't think I like your tone. What are you insinuating?"

We had to laugh as we were so content in our relationship that the both of us had gained a little weight but had tried hard over the summer to lose it.

"Did I tell you, Babe? Robb sent me an update on the cruise entertainment and Mario Cantone is going to be the headliner comedy act."

"Wow, that'll be cool. He's so funny."

"Yeah, and some of the other performers on the ship

are Shann Carr and Michael Holmes. Shann is from Palm Springs …stand-up comic … very funny."

"I recognize the name Shann, but not sure who Michael Holmes is."

"'The Judy Show.' Remember we saw him perform at Martini's Above Fourth last summer?"

"Oh of course, that was a lot of fun, an amazing show. He's from Palm Springs too isn't he?"

"Yeah, he is. With so many performers from Palm Springs on the ship, it's even more likely John and Craig will be on this cruise as well. It would be great to see them again."

Driving into the long term parking area at the Large Ships harbor, you couldn't miss seeing our ship docked, ready for departure on the high seas. The *Serendipity* looked huge and majestic moored there in the harbor. For me, being in this parking lot at the Large Ships pier brought back bittersweet memories. It was just over a year ago that I worked the case of the murder of a dear friend of mine and in the course of that investigation, was held hostage right here in a warehouse building off the pier. I nearly lost my life with that assignment but in the end I solved the murder mystery and came away with a sizeable bonus that was financing this trip for the two of us.

The day was here and we were both excited to be going on such a fun vacation together. The *Serendipity of the Seas* is the largest ship that can squeeze through the locks of the Panama Canal. That part of the cruise would be an experience unto itself. It's hard to imagine how this all works and it's something I've always wanted to witness.

We parked the car and hopped on the shuttle bus to the customs area. We discovered a huge maze of people all thrilled to be getting on this big ship for the next ten days. We said good-bye to our luggage as it was whisked away to be delivered, hopefully, to our stateroom. The check-in process moved relatively fast considering the thousands of guests boarding the ship. Approaching the gangway, we had our first photo snap taken by the ship's photographer -- with many more photos to follow.

The excitement in the air was ridiculously prevalent. Everyone was in a party mood. We didn't recognize anyone in the crowd but it was like everyone was a friend. As we waited on the upper pool deck overlooking the boarding area, the Reggae music from the steel pans band played on and the complimentary yellow bird cocktails flowed to keep us all in the mood. It would be something like two hours before we were allowed to go to our stateroom and get settled in -- happily, with our luggage waiting for us.

We'd been surprised when we checked in before

boarding to learn that our friend and travel agency owner, Robb, had upgraded us to a suite with an outdoor balcony. We'd booked a room with a window but the balcony was a delightful and romantic touch. Leave it to Robb to go the extra mile to make sure we'd have a memorable vacation. We were also surprised upon entering our suite to see a large basket of tropical flowers, fresh fruit and a bottle of champagne. The card read, *"Thanks, guys, for your business. Enjoy your cruise. Bon Voyage, Robb, ExtaSea Cruises."* How thoughtful and what a great way to start our romantic get-away.

As we unpacked our bags, there were several announcements over the PA system including one from the Captain who introduced himself to the passengers. In his broken English with what appeared to be a German accent, he began: *"Ladies and Gentlemen, this is your Captain, Fritz Stubing."* We had to laugh thinking we were on the Love Boat.

"On behalf of the Serendipity of the Seas, *I want to welcome you all aboard. ...Before we leave the dock, it's mandatory that all passengers attend a lifeboat muster in the unlikely event of an emergency at sea. In just about an hour from now you will hear seven short horn blasts followed by one long one, indicating you are to report to your lifeboat station with your life vests for further emergency instructions. Once we have completed the lifeboat drill, we will be departing for the high seas. Thank you!"*

How exciting, we are actually doing this, I thought. The next hour waiting to leave the docks passed quickly as we explored the deck and imbibed in the welcome-aboard cocktails being served.

When we heard the lifeboat drill begin with the blasts of the ship's horn, we did as we'd been told and reported to our assigned area, hoping like hell we'd never have to actually use this information. It was still necessary to know before we departed. Once the lifeboat drill was completed, we dropped off our life vests back in our stateroom and assembled on the upper deck to wave good-bye to the many friends and family on the dock. We didn't want to miss any part of the embarkation party. Inundated by streamers, music and noise makers, we felt the ship pull away from the dock and watched the land we were leaving behind get farther and farther away until we could see nothing of it any longer. We were now at sea.

4

A Floating City

We were excited to check out all the amenities of this fabulous floating city that would be our home for the next ten days. At the center of the ship where we first entered was a seven story atrium with mezzanine balcony vantage points at each floor. Great for people watching!

The focal point of the atrium was the seven story tall water feature, a tube of water that bubbled much like that of the old lava lamps we all had during our college days. This feature, however, was pretty awesome, being amazingly tall and with a rainbow of alternating colored lights accentuating the bubbles. I looked forward to sitting in a plush lounge chair at one of the many levels or perched on a stool at one of two lounge bars and sipping a cocktail while watching the swirling bubbles rise. That would be mesmerizing.

We ventured out on the sports deck to observe the pool and recreation area. Besides the outdoor and indoor pools and spa, we discovered a wave pool outdoors for board surfing. We walked around like two children discovering Disneyland for the first time. We found the rock climbing wall and Brad challenged me to a climb later in the week. Not being much of an adventurer, I secretly hoped that might be so much "later" that maybe I wouldn't have to actually go through with the challenge.

We found the formal dining room that had a mezzanine level overlooking the main floor, clearly designed to replicate the Titanic, grand stair case and all --- and we'd been told there were three other intimate dining restaurants on board. And of course several bars tucked away throughout the ship. We found two of the restaurants, one Italian cuisine and one American Bistro. I still wanted to locate the French Café restaurant, but there would be plenty of time over the next ten days.

We walked past the gym located at the back of the ship -- or should I say aft part of the ship. It was on one of the upper levels and the walls facing out towards the back were all glass -- allowing for an awesome view while working out on the treadmill or Precor machines. We noticed an aerobic schedule posted and I told Brad with all the gourmet food and delicious desserts, I should probably move in to the gym. I was determined to enjoy the cruise, but also wanted to try and keep off the few extra pounds I'd lost before we left home.

The gym had the men's private Jacuzzi and steam room as well as spa treatments by appointment for services such as facials, sea weed wrap and of course massage of various types. They all sounded like something we would have to take advantage of, regardless of the cost. This vacation was meant to be enjoyed.

We decided to stop and have a cocktail at the pool bar before heading back to our room to get ready for dinner that evening.

Dinner the first night was casual, thankfully, as we were both a little tired from the events of the day. We would be meeting our assigned dining mates for the duration of the cruise for the first time. We had signed up for the late seating for dinner and requested a table of six people. We hadn't adjusted to the idea of late dining and we were dressed and ready to go at least an hour early. We decided to check out the main dining deck to see about finding a bar to grab a before-dinner drink.

We found a really nice gentlemen's piano bar close to the dining room called Acqua Pazza. It was a perfect way to relax before dinner even though the name had us a little concerned -- Acqua Pazza meaning "crazy waters" in Italian. We enjoyed the relaxing piano music performed by the talented Joel Baker. This was to become our ritual every evening before and sometimes after dinners, listening to Joel tickle the ivories. They also had an open-mic night with wanna-be performers from the room taking the spotlight and microphone to perform …sometimes good and sometimes not so good, but always entertaining.

Finishing up our martinis, we heard the dinner call tone over the PA system and headed into the dining room. As we approached our table, another couple walked up so we began the introduction process. The older gentleman of the two I guessed to be in his 70's, while his traveling companion looked to be in his 30's.

The older gentleman stretched out his hand. "Hello, guys, I guess we're dining with you. My name is Bill." I shook his hand. "And this is my partner, Jayde."

Bill came across as being a wealthy man with his starched oxford cloth shirt sporting monogrammed cuffs. His hands were adorned with diamond rings and I couldn't help noticing the classic two-color Gucci watch on his wrist. It was obvious that Bill was the "sugar daddy" in this relationship.

Bill's partner was a tall skinny young man wearing a tux shirt that was cut off at the midriff exposing his gaunt mid-section. His low rise jeans were worn low enough to show just a hint of pubic hair. "That's Jayde with a 'y,'" the young man blurted out and extended his limp-wristed hand with black-painted finger nails. *"Enchante."* I wasn't sure if I was supposed to kiss his hand or shake it but I opted for the traditional manly hand shake.

He was definitely a colorful individual. On one side of his head, his hair was cropped to a fraction of an inch, while the other side displayed about five inches of jet black straight hair that fell over his right eye. To clear this shock of hair from his eyes, he would continually flick his head, tossing his locks temporarily aside. After exchanging names we all sat down. It looked like we would have another couple joining us since we were seated at a table for six.

"Jayde and I are from Chicago. Are you guys from California? Seems to be a lot of California guys on the ship."

"Yes, Bill, we live in San Diego so we didn't have far to go to catch the ship."

My eye was drawn to the pendant on a gold chain around his neck. "Excuse me, Bill, is that a Krugerrand?" He was wearing what looked like an African Krugerrand.

"Yes, Tony, thank you for noticing. I picked this up in Johannesburg on a photo safari …maybe thirty years ago now. It's a favorite of mine."

"Well, it's very nice. I can see why you favor it." The Krugerrand is a pure gold coin first minted in South Africa in 1967, he explained. Currently their existence is rare and valuable.

Our waiter brought our menus and within minutes another couple joined us. They were both fairly young -- likely in their 30's. Almost immediately, we noticed the sign language communication between them. The taller one introduced himself as Steve, and his friend as Frankie, saying that his friend spoke only in sign language. Steve too, apparently had a hearing problem, as he spoke with a dialect that was hard to understand. When he turned his head to acknowledge his friend, I noticed the cochlear implant on the left side of his head. It struck me that this could be challenging since neither Brad nor I know any sign language.

While looking over the menu, Bill and Jayde began to argue about something concerning the menu. Their voices raised and demeanor was hostile toward each other until Jayde finally dismissed Bill and turned away. We noticed Jayde constantly checking out other men who passed our table and cruising the wait staff. If not for holding a casual conversation with Bill, Brad and I might just as well be dining alone. Right after the appetizer course, Jayde stood up to excuse himself from the table but it was unclear exactly where he was headed. Bill seemed to be annoyed by his sudden departure and gave Jayde a look of disappointment. I figured Jayde had caught the eye of someone and was headed for a hook-up in the men's room.

As he walked away from our table, I couldn't help but notice the *"tramp stamp"* tattoo on the small of his back. I pondered the thought of how many other tattoos or piercings this young man might have on his body.

Our entrees were delivered, and a few minutes after

that Jayde returned. He and Bill got into another of their apparently frequent arguments as Bill questioned Jayde as to where he had gone.

Bill said, "Well, that was rude. Are you going to join us for dinner? Where did you go?"

Jayde was clearly irritated with this interrogation and snapped back to Bill, "None of your business but if you must know, I had to use the restroom." The elevated voices caused some heads to turn and Brad and I felt uncomfortable with this public display. They continued to bicker with snide remarks the rest of the evening although they softened the volume somewhat. Steve and Frankie didn't seem to be bothered by any of this since they could only observe the body language for the most part.

As we finished up with dinner and left the dining room, I looked at Brad and knew that both of us were thinking the same thing. "I don't think I can handle that every night, Brad. We might be dining in one of the other restaurants this week or the pool-side buffet."

Brad sighed and remarked sarcastically, "Wasn't that enjoyable? ...Maybe we can see about getting reassigned to another table or something."

∽

The next morning we woke early after a very relaxing sleep. The ever so slight rocking motion of the ship had

had the same effect on our tired bodies as a cradle has on a baby.

I decided I wanted to hit the gym for aerobics while Brad headed out to participate in the Walk Around, a jogging and walking track for an organized daily exercise program. The aerobics was a very basic class, but at least I was getting some exercise and worked up a bit of sweat. I could probably have done just as well on the treadmill.

After aerobics I decided to shower and sit in the steam room for a bit. The locker room facilities were very clean and nice and at this time of the morning, it was pretty quiet. I wrapped a towel around me and entered the dark cave of the steam room, unable to see much of anything. I waited a few seconds to let my eyes adjust and for some of the steam to dissipate before taking a spot on an upper bench area. Spreading my towel, I lay down to just relax. The warm steam felt so rejuvenating after my aerobic workout. The solace and darkness of the room helped me to relax and meditate. I felt mentally transported to a state of nirvana.

I could hear the door to the steam room open and close several times as guys came and went, but it was pretty quiet and relaxing for the most part. Then as I lay there half asleep, I began to hear an all too familiar sound. It was a slurping of sorts and I knew what was going on. Someone was getting a blow job right there in the steam room. I lay there listening to the erotic sounds and soon the slurping was accompanied by moaning. I began to get aroused and my cock started to stiffen at the thought of this blow job taking place in the darkness just feet away from me. The more I listened the harder I got until I was sporting a full on erection.

The moaning began to intensify and as the steam started to clear, I could make out the images on the lower bench, with one of the two guys on his knees in front of the other who was seated. The sounds became almost an outburst of ecstasy as the one guy reached climax and shot his load. The moaning then became a sigh …a sigh of contentment and release. It wasn't long after that I heard the door open again as someone exited the room. The steam started to build again to a point where I couldn't make out images any longer.

As I lay there relaxed with my semi-hard cock beginning to go completely flaccid once again, I suddenly felt a hand caressing my groin area. I was shocked and curious to know who this mysterious nympho man was. I laid there not knowing what to do. I was enjoying his touch and he knew how to stimulate arousal -- his hands on my penis felt nice. I found the eroticism of not knowing who was fondling me arousing and my cock quickly stiffened once again in his hands. My guilt, however, made me sit up to pull away. I was in a committed relationship with a man that I dearly loved and would never want to jeopardize that. I looked down in the clearing of the steam and I recognized the familiar black fingernail polish. It was Jayde. No wonder his relationship with Bill was a rocky one.

I left the steam room immediately and hoped that Jayde didn't even realize who it was that he had been fondling. But either way, I expected things would be a little uncomfortable at dinner that evening. I related some of the steam room experience to Brad, leaving out certain details, of course, that would serve no purpose other than to possibly damage our near perfect relationship and put a cloud over our romantic cruise.

∽

As the day went on, the seas began to get choppy with some pretty large swells. I was feeling a little bit queasy but hanging out at the pool with the fresh air seemed to help. The Captain's announcement was comforting as well.

*"Ladies and gentlemen, this is your Captain speaking. I apologize for the rough seas we are currently experiencing. I can assure you once we get beyond the Baja land mass and out into deeper waters further from the shore, it should calm down. **'Still waters run deep.'** In the meantime, relax with a cocktail."*

5

Forming New Bonds

After spending an exhausting afternoon poolside and enjoying several of the "cocktails of the day" while listening to the steel pan music, Brad and I were really starting to relax and get into the laid back atmosphere of the ship. We dressed for dinner early once again and headed down to our favorite piano bar outside the dining room for yet another cocktail.

When it was time for dinner, we reluctantly headed to our table in the dining room, as we both dreaded another evening with our dining mates. We figured the next evening we would try to arrange dinner alone in one of the private dining restaurants. As we neared our table, we were approached by the maître de. "Excusez moi. Messieurs Felice and Fisher ...follow me, s'il vous plait."

I looked to Brad and he shrugged his shoulders, both of us puzzled. What was this about? Had we done something wrong? Following the French gentleman towards the Grand Staircase to the upper mezzanine level of dining, he stopped and turned to us. "I hope you don't mind, but I've taken the liberty of assigning you both to a more …suitable dining table." And with a wink of his eye, he turned and we followed him upstairs.

The mezzanine dining room was quite elegant. We were enjoying the atmosphere already. We were led to a table for eight with four guys already seated. As we focused on one of the couples, we realized these were the two guys from Palm Springs, John and Craig, who we had met some time ago at a cocktail party.

"Hey guys, what a pleasant surprise." John was already standing to greet us.

Craig stood up and the four of us hugged. "So good to see you guys. I can't believe it. …So you're joining our table for dinner?"

"I guess we are."

"Bon appetite!" And with that, the maître de turned and left.

This would be such a better dining experience as well as a fun opportunity to connect with former acquaintances. We'd had a hunch we may run into John and Craig on this cruise, but now to be dining with them was more than we could have hoped for.

"Excuse me, guys," John interrupted to get our attention. "Let me introduce you to our friends from Palm Springs. They enjoy cruising as much as or more so than Craig and I do. This is Randy and his husband Kevin."

From the place setting, it appeared that two others would be joining us, but there was only one additional chair at the table. I guess this was part of my private investigator training coming out in me to observe a detail like this, but I found it curious. It wasn't long before my curiosity was satisfied. We had just started to discuss some of the evening's menu items when the final couple joined us at the table. A rather tall, muscular, middle-aged man with a shaved head maneuvered another gentleman in a wheelchair up to the table and proceeded to get him settled in. We allowed him some time to complete his routine without interruptions before we introduced ourselves.

"Good evening. I'm Tony and this is my partner, Brad." I stood and extended a hand shake.

"Nice to meet you. I'm Jack and this is Bruce." He nodded towards his friend in the wheelchair. "You guys enjoying the cruise so far?"

"Very much so …and you two as well?"

We continued with the small talk for a while but I was intrigued about this couple and wanted to know more. "So, Jack, how long have you and Bruce been together?" I asked.

"Oh, we're not a couple …just close friends. Bruce hires me on occasion to assist him with traveling."

"Wow. That works out well for the both of you. I just thought you were together and from the looks of the muscles in your arms, it appears that you have a lot of experience working with Bruce and that wheelchair."

"Ha!" Jack chuckled. "No, these 'guns' are from working out and from my real job."

Now being even more interested, I asked Jack what it is that he does for a living. "I'm a massage therapist in Palm Springs. …A legitimate massage therapist that is."

Brad and I were really enjoying the conversation and forming new friendships and bonds with these guys. We were all around the same age and had similar backgrounds. I wondered about Bruce and his confinement to the wheelchair but was hesitant to ask him about it for fear it may be an uncomfortable conversation for him. At a later point in the evening, Bruce gave me a lead-in to ask him further questions about his disability -- referring to a prior time in his life when his mobility was not restricted.

"So Bruce, how long have you been using a wheelchair to get around?" I sensed a scowl from Brad after the words came out of my mouth. "…I hope you don't mind me asking," I added.

"No, not at all, Tony. It's been about seven years now for me. It's been quite an adjustment since I was always such an avid nudist and loved frequenting the nude beaches. They do make special beach wheelchairs but that's such a hassle."

I felt bad for Bruce as you could tell he missed his

former life and the freedom to maneuver on his own without the burden of this chair. I thought about how difficult it would be for me to give up going to the beach. "Sorry to hear that, Bruce." I didn't know what else I could say.

"It's not all that bad. There are worse things in life so I consider myself pretty fortunate, to tell the truth. The most frustrating thing for me is the way that this all came about."

It appeared that Bruce was actually enjoying the opportunity to talk about the experience and what had brought him to this stage in his life.

Before I had a chance to ask, Brad spoke up. "If you don't mind me asking, Bruce, what did happen to you?" Brad was now curious too.

"I came down with a really severe, life threatening case of Guillain-Barre' syndrome. I nearly died."

I cringed at the thought. "Wow, that's terrible. I didn't realize Guillain-Barre' was that serious."

"It can be and in my case it was just about as bad as it can get. I'm just thankful I have such a good friendship with Jack who helps me get around and offers me companionship."

We all seemed to become closer during that conversation, and I looked forward to becoming friends with these new acquaintances as well. As the eight of us prepared to leave the table, John asked, "So is anyone planning to see 'The Judy Show' tonight?"

"That's Michael Holmes from Palm Springs, right?" I said.

John appeared to be pretty knowledgeable of the entertainment aboard the ship. "Yes, 'The Judy Show' will run tonight and again later in the week. It's a great show. Craig and I have seen him perform several times before."

"Yes, we know of his show. Brad and I saw him perform in San Diego once a long time ago at Martini's Above Fourth. It was a great performance."

"Well, if you want to join us, we're meeting up with Randy and Kevin just outside the Cabaret Theater before the show on the right hand side of the theater entrance. …And how about you guys, Jack?"

Jack was preparing to wheel Bruce away from the table. "I'll check with Bruce later and we might meet you there. But Bruce usually likes to be in bed by about ten o'clock. Then I go out to play and can usually be found in the casino or the dance club."

"Brad and I will meet you guys outside the theater before the show. Thanks for the enjoyable dinner company."

John chuckled, "It was a pleasure. And so glad we met up with you. We'll look for you later this evening at the show."

∽

The morning sun was flooding our stateroom from our patio slider and we could feel the ship was not moving. At some time during the night we'd docked in Puerto Vallarta. It was very early but we knew we wanted to get some breakfast and take some time exploring the city sights. We'd made plans for later in the afternoon to meet up with John and Craig and possibly Randy and Kevin at Blue Chairs Beach bar and have some cocktails and enjoy the scenery. Every gay man visiting Puerto Vallarta ends up on Blue Chairs Beach eventually.

We planned to check out the shopping at Gringo Gulch and stroll along the beach walk down in Old Town. Brad also wanted to show me the two hillside condo resort rentals that he owns in town. Until very recently, I had no idea that Brad had this investment in this resort city. The subject had come up unexpectedly one night over dinner with our good friends, Cris and Michael. He invited the two of them to vacation with us some time in Puerto Vallarta saying we could all stay in his two bedroom condo. That came as quite a shock to me.

Now seeing the complex for the first time where his properties are located, I was very impressed. It's a gated complex above Old Town Puerto Vallarta and looks as if it had been built during the late 90s. The complex is nothing like you'd see in most parts of Mexico. The construction looks more like something we might find in San Diego.

"Wow, Brad, this is really beautiful. And the view from up here, very nice! I had no idea." It seemed that

Brad had done pretty well with investing his money.

"Thanks. Glad you like it. We can vacation here any time. Just say the word."

"I'd like to come here with Cris and Michael like we talked about. That would be fun some time."

"Sure thing. We need to plan on that with them. Now, Hon, have you seen enough of the city sights and shopping? Ready to hit the beach?"

"Sounds good to me. I could use a cocktail and some 'eye candy.'"

We headed down to Playa de los Muertos Beach to meet up with John and Craig and planned to all walk from there to Blue Chairs Beach. As we approached them, we could see several packages in their possession.

"Looks like you picked up a few souvenirs," Brad said to them facetiously.

"Well, you know how it is, have to buy for friends back home and support the local economy. Did you guys have a good morning?"

"Yes, very much so and it looks like you two had a productive day as well. ...So are we going to wait for Randy and Kevin? Do you know if they're going to make it?"

John spoke up, "They're going to meet us at the Blue Chairs Beach."

And with that we headed out walking south along the beach where we could just barely see the smattering of blue chairs in the distance.

I love being at the beach and especially back home at Black's where I can shed my clothes and enjoy the freedom that comes with that feeling. This last summer I hadn't found much time to get away to the beach so I was enjoying this walk along the water's edge digging my toes into the cold, wet sand with every step. I have a thing for the smell of the ocean in the air and the seagulls swarming in flight overhead diving down towards the beachgoers. I was recalling so many fond memories of living in San Diego and now to have new memories with Brad and our new friendships, I was feeling overjoyed and without a care or worry.

6

Beach Memories

The beach was packed with tourists. There were two cruise ships docked at the same time at the pier, so many of the guys that we saw and didn't recognize were likely from the other, smaller ship.

As we approached the Blue Chairs, we could see Randy standing and waving to us to catch our attention. He and Kevin had secured six chairs beneath two palapas, protected from the intense sun. In Mexico, we soon learned, a palapa was a thatched roof umbrella or shelter from the sun. Getting situated, we were quickly greeted by a cocktail waiter from the bar, asking if he could take a drink order for us.

"I am so ready for a drink and a little R&R on the beach," I said. I realized how exhausted I was from all the walking we'd done. "I'll have a margarita, rocks, no salt, and a goblet of shrimp ceviche."

Brad paused in thought and then growled, "Yum, that sounds good, I'll have the same."

John and Craig spoke up, "Make that four."

We were enjoying the endless parade of Speedo clad men on the beach in front of us while watching the parasailing. The pilot boats brought the adventurous few dangerously close to the high rise hotels upon landing. Brad and I kept resisting the beach vendors selling their knick-knack crafts on the beach while John and Craig delighted with a bargain and bringing home a few more souvenirs from the beach.

At one point I noticed Jayde in his skimpy see-thru shorts strutting along the water's edge, working the crowd. Bill was nowhere to be seen and Jayde was certainly acting like he hoped to get lucky and pick up someone at the beach.

Even more entertaining for us as the afternoon wore on was checking out the Mexican call-boys in their thong bikinis flaunting their waif-like effeminate bodies on the beach. Looking to score a quick trick with some of the tourists and make a few bucks, they really knew how to work their audience and appeared to be getting some business. Mostly older men would stop and talk with them and then we'd notice them walk off the beach back to one of the hotels along the beachfront.

After a few hours on the beach and three margaritas, we started to contemplate the trek back to the ship for embarkation. Our ship wasn't leaving port until six o'clock but we didn't want to be late. Suddenly we noticed the Mexican Policia running down the beach towards the Blue Chairs. Almost simultaneously we heard a commotion back by the beach bar and we stood up to get a better look. I decided to walk over closer and that was when I realized the policia had Jayde restrained and another man was talking to them. It appeared there'd been some altercation between them and the police had been called. I thought I recognized the other guy in the squabble as someone from our ship as well. It seemed that wherever Jayde went, he managed to create a ruckus and attract attention.

Back in our state room I took my shower and was relaxing on the balcony before getting dressed. I loved that Brad and I were so comfortable with each other that we could both lounge and spend time together naked. It was very natural and comfortable for both of us.

"Hey, Babe, are you going to jump in the shower? Remember we told the guys we'd meet them for a drink before dinner at Acqua Pazza."

Brad rolled over on the bed and sat up. "Yeah, I'm going."

He walked out to the balcony and bent over me from behind, as I sat in my lounge chair. His hands grouped my chest and he kissed my cheek. I responded to his affection as I usually did with a growing woody. "If you keep that up we won't make it to dinner, let alone cocktails."

I could feel the tingling in my groin as my cock continued to stiffen. "Go ... get in the shower ...NOW!" Brad reached down and gave my semi-hard cock a quick squeeze and then went inside to take his shower.

I sat there enjoying the tropical breeze and the view of the horizon and reflected upon my life -- about how well things had been going for me over the last couple of years. Managing a reputable and prominent private investigating business was a goal of mine I'd achieved.

My love life and relationship with Brad could hardly have been any better. We'd had a couple of years to test our compatibility, and I was having thoughts about taking it to the next step now that gay marriage was legal in California and recognized by our government. But for the time being I was content with our commitment to one another and waiting to see what the future might bring.

We met up with John and Craig and Randy and Kevin in the bar for a quick drink before dinner. Joel was playing a medley of show tunes and we hated to leave the entertainment, but the dinner tone was announcing the second seating for dinner. Approaching our table, we could see Bruce and Jack had already arrived and were contemplating the menu. This evening's special theme was American Bistro cuisine and I zeroed in on the surf and turf. That was an easy decision for me.

"Has anyone booked a massage at the fitness spa

yet?" I was looking forward to taking advantage of a professional, relaxing massage.

"Maybe we could do a couples massage?" Brad looked at me with his sexy grin and a raised eyebrow.

"Craig and I talked about that too. It sounds nice and I enjoy being pampered."

"You guys don't have to spend that kind of money for a good massage," said Jack. "I can give you a relaxing all-over massage for about half of what they charge." It sounded like he was volunteering his services.

"And take it from me, guys, he's really good," said Bruce. "Strong hands! I have him work me over once a week." Bruce had high praise for Jack's expertise as a massage therapist.

"Well, I might just take you up on that, Jack."

After finishing dinner we made plans to all meet up outside the Marquis Theater for the late night show featuring Mario Cantone. Shann Carr was the opening comic act and everyone agreed she is well worth seeing, putting on a really good performance. Even Bruce and Jack decided to make a late night of it and join us for the show. It was looking to be a fun evening with new friendships in the making.

7

Ship Adventures

Despite the busy day we'd had and then staying up late the previous evening, Brad and I both woke up early the next morning. We were somewhere at sea south of Puerto Vallarta. And we were determined to exercise before meeting up for breakfast. So I headed out to my aerobics class with plans to take my shower later, after my workout. Brad put on his walking shoes for laps around the ship's jogging deck.

Later, Brad and I met for breakfast at the poolside café and made plans for our day at sea. The daily news leaflet that was distributed outlined the various activities. Brad decided he wanted to go to the Art Auction and I was looking forward to some lounge time in the sun. It was common knowledge that the uppermost deck at the bow of the ship was a nude sunbathing deck. I wanted to check that out and relax with a good book and take a nap.

After breakfast, I said a quick goodbye to Brad and

gave him a kiss and reminded him not to spend too much at the auction. I know how he can get carried away with finding a bargain.

I gathered my supplies for some sun time, and found my way to the upper deck bow where there were dozens of empty lounge chairs. There were maybe a half dozen guys scattered around, mostly nude but some with suits on as well. I found a quiet, out of the way location with good exposure to the sun and staked out a lounge chair.

It felt good to shed my clothes outdoors and to feel the gentle ocean breezes caressing the hair on my body. It was very stimulating at first and I found myself getting aroused. I laid out my towel and put on my Maui Jim's in preparation for reading a good book and possibly dozing off in the sun. My semi-hard cock quickly went flaccid again and I kicked back to relax.

After about an hour with no one else joining the few au naturel sun worshippers, I was starting to nod off. The book in my hands kept falling onto my chest and I was about to give it up and not fight it any longer.

I came to life rather quickly however when a tall, tanned, blond, handsome man walked onto the deck area looking for a place to settle. He was probably in his early 30's, with sun-bleached hairy legs and hairy chest. The tanning lotion that covered his body made his body hair glisten in the sun. I was getting hard just watching him clothed let alone envisioning a possible strip down.

After surveying the deck and the few guys there, most of them sleeping, he headed back to where I was sprawled buck naked on my lounge. He located a chair only a few feet away from me and directly in my line of sight. I was wide awake now and my dark glasses worked well to hide my stares as I pretended to be reading.

He laid the lounge chair flat, spread out his towel, and stripped off his Hawaiian Board shorts. He had no tan line which was expected. I couldn't help stare at the rather large uncut cock that hung between his legs and the set of full, ample balls that supported it. I instantly began to get hard watching him, and he knew I was enjoying the show and not interested in reading.

He settled down on his stomach with his firm round buttocks exposed. His butt cheeks were covered with a bit of fine blond hair that was driving me crazy. I wasn't sure I was going to be able to lay there so close to him without embarrassing myself.

Every now and then he'd look up to make sure I was still enjoying the view. He began to squirm slowly and the muscles in his butt cheeks pulsed. He was putting on a show for me and I loved it without a doubt. Keeping a close eye on him, I suddenly realized the head of his cock was growing out from under him facing me and then he rolled slightly to make sure I wouldn't miss anything. He was rock hard now lying on his cock and I could see a bit of pre cum at the head.

By this time there was no way to hide my erection except possibly with the book I was holding, but had stopped reading once he arrived. Watching him wriggling on his towel, his cock seemed to grow ever larger and harder. Finally, he looked up at me and smiled, rolling over on his back. His beautiful hard cock now standing straight up, he reached for some suntan lotion and began to rub it all over his cock and balls. My eyes were locked on him as he stroked, moving the ample foreskin of his cock forward and back in slow steady motions.

I wanted so badly to approach him and touch his perfect body and hard cock. Just watching this exhibition had me totally aroused. I could almost shoot a load without even touching myself. I could tell he was into showing-off for me and his low moaning let me know that. For me the fact that all this was taking place without anyone else even realizing it was very erotic.

His moaning now turned into a gasp and I could tell he was near to shooting his load. Then, a complete euphoria of an eruption of thick white sperm spewed all over his muscled chest. The contrast of his tanned skin and the dappled white cum nearly brought me to orgasm as well. His body still tense from the ejaculation, he exhaled with a sigh of release. His body seemed to instantly go limp. He rolled over onto his stomach again, looked up at me one last time and smiled and settled in for a nap.

After this performance, I was far from ready to sleep and wanted to head back to our stateroom and have mad passionate sex with my man. I was disappointed when I returned to find that Brad was still out. I stripped down naked and sprawled face-down on the bed with my legs spread. I could still see the guy on the lounge chair, fuzzy ass in the air, tanned, muscled chest, stroking his cock to climax, for me to watch and enjoy.

The sliding door to the balcony was open and I could hear the sound of the waves lapping against the hull of the ship as it cut through the water. The gentle rocking motion was hypnotic and the clean fresh sea air mixed with the sweet smell of plumeria flowers in the tropical arrangement in our room was like euphoria from a drug, overtaking my reverie.

Just as I started to drift off to sleep I heard the rattling of the door handle. I wanted Brad to attack me as I lay there still, with my ass end up. Suddenly I started to question in my mind if this was Brad or if perhaps our cabin steward was coming around to deliver fresh squeezed juice and a refill of our ice bucket. I lay still, pretending to be asleep. The room was quiet. Then I heard the click of the *"do not disturb"* lock. I knew what was about to happen and I was so ready for Brad to make love to me. I smiled at the thought.

I felt Brad moving from the foot of the bed making

his way up my legs, exploring my body every inch of the way. I could feel his warm breath on my ass and his hands caressing my buttocks. His naked body pressing against my backside felt good. The head of his cock rubbed against my ass and I could feel his pre cum. I began to gyrate my hips and groin, making sure he knew what I wanted. I couldn't wait to feel his cock inside me, thrusting and pounding my ass.

Brad nibbled and whispered in my ear, "You are so fucking hot. You drive me crazy." All I could do was moan with anticipation of him making love to me.

Brad flipped me over onto my back and straddled me with his sexy muscular body, now taut from the surge of testosterone. Pulling him closer, I was even more aroused by the feel of his hairy buttocks. He began to kiss me passionately. He continued moving down my chest, kissing and biting at my nipples. "Oh yea, work those nipples. …Mm, feels good! …Suck on them. Yeah!" Brad continued working his way down my chest, licking my stomach and finally reaching my engorged cock and swallowing it in his hot mouth. It felt so good, I could barely contain myself and nearly shot my load right there.

I continued thrusting my groin in sync with his sucking and was totally enjoying the feeling of my cock in his warm mouth. We were both close to climax now. Brad pulled away and reached over me to the bedside table, grabbing a tube of KY. Raising my legs in the air to position my ass for penetration, he lubed his cock and then fingered my ass with gel. The massaging of my prostate nearly brought me to climax once again.

I moaned, "Mm, yeah, I want that cock inside me."

"Oh, damn. ...I love you so much, sexy man. Take this." And with that he slid his cock inside me and began to thrust, pounding me hard. With some lube I stroked my cock as he fucked my ass. I was in a complete state of exhilaration, but held back my climax until I could feel Brad getting ready to shoot his load. He was getting close, I could tell. The muscles in his chest tightened and his face reddened. The veins in his neck now were becoming well-defined and his legs tensed up and clamped like a vice around my body. Suddenly his body shuddered with a powerful release of an orgasm. I could feel him shoot inside me -- and with that, my load of cum, that had been building up ever since the show I enjoyed earlier, shot all over my chest and above my head onto the pillow.

We clung together there for several minutes, relaxing in the afterglow of hot sex, not saying a word. Finally Brad said, "Damn, you are so sexy, Hon. And what a load you had there."

"That was so hot, Babe. You have no idea how much I needed that. I love you so much."

"Believe me, when I walked in the door and saw that sexy tight ass waiting for me, I knew how much you needed to be made love to. That was really sweet."

We lay there side by side in bed, enjoying the moment. Breathing in the fresh air and listening to the ocean, letting our bodies return to normal, we drifted off into a restful nap.

~

That evening was the Captain's dinner and Brad and I looked dapper in our tuxes. The menu for the night featured Scandinavian cuisine, in honor of the ship's registry. I knew I'd have to work out extra hard in the morning after this meal.

We'd not yet been able to attend one of the lavish Midnight Buffets because we were usually still full from dinner, but we decided this was the night we would make time for that. With all the elaborate ice sculptures and butter figurines accenting the endless tables of desserts and finger food, it was a must-see just for pictures if not to eat.

We hadn't had a chance to visit the casino yet either and so tonight was our chance in our tuxes to do a sort of James Bond appearance there. With a martini in hand we could play the part until we placed our meager bets on the craps table or the roulette wheel. It was fun to dress up and, after our passionate love making earlier in the day, Brad and I both had a certain glow about us.

Jack had mentioned that he could usually be found

in the casino in the evenings, and we spotted him as we made our way through the crowd. He'd helped Bruce settle in for the evening and was enjoying his free time for himself. We went over to say hello and watch him play. His gambling style was a little out of our league and our eyes widened as we watched him place thousand dollar bets.

"Damn, can't afford that," I whispered to Brad making sure it wasn't overheard by Jack.

That's when Brad chose to lean over and whisper back into my ear, "Hon, I bought a painting at the auction today."

I was the conservative one with money in the relationship and Brad liked nice things. I was always trying to keep him from spending so much. "Oh my god, what did you buy?"

Guiltily now Brad said, "I think you'll like it and it was a good bargain."

"Okay Babe, what is it, what did you buy?"

"It's an original Erte. Once it's framed, it will look fantastic hanging over the fireplace. The colors are in gray tones with black and burgundy. It should be great in our home."

Brad seemed so excited, like a little boy with a new toy. And I liked the way he referred to it as "our home." All I could do was smile at him and look forward to seeing his purchase that was being shipped to "our home."

8

Disaster at Sea

The next day we woke up with the ship docked at our next port of call, Acapulco. Brad and I had talked with the guys about our plans for a side trip or excursion while in Acapulco, but Jack and Bruce had opted out to do something on their own. Since the other six of us had at some time in our lives visited the city, we decided to do something a little more adventurous and avoid the City Tour. We planned to spend the day on an excursion to a private island, Tortuga del Mar, located about a mile from shore. There we could enjoy snorkeling among the sea life and swimming with the sea turtles. The day included cocktails and lunch and a lot of relaxation in the sun and sand.

A van picked us up at the pier and drove us to a catamaran waiting about 30 minutes away. The boat then carried about a dozen guys from shore to the Island. There we spent the day exploring the island and snorkeling as much as we wanted. Being a group of gay men far away from any other civilization, it didn't take long before the swimsuits came off and we were all enjoying the day au naturel.

With Brad swimming naked beside me, I felt like one of the young lovers from Blue Lagoon. The water was so clear and azure you could see the bottom nearly a hundred feet below. What a wonderful bonding experience this was as we formed new friendships with John and Craig as well as Randy and Kevin.

My meditating thoughts while lying half asleep and nude on this beautiful white sandy beach drifted to recall my conversation with Blaine earlier. When he called in the spring we'd made plans to visit Black's Beach before the end of the summer once he'd relocated. Apparently his plans changed or possibly he'd postponed his planned move to San Diego. I'd looked forward to having him in town to spend more time with Brad and myself and to have a beach buddy since it was more difficult for Brad to get time away from his teaching during the week.

By early afternoon, we'd all worked up an appetite in the sea and sun, and couldn't wait for the tour's lunch feast fit for a king. The buffet table was spread with bowls of shrimp, calamari, Mahi-Mahi, and other tropical fish. There were plates of pineapple, coconut, papaya and tropical fruit I had never experienced before. We enjoyed sipping the drink of the day -- a pink mojito

-- and after two of them I could feel a buzz. It was a very memorable day for all of us. I was feeling melancholy as we headed back to the ship but this was something I would always cherish from the trip and an experience that would bond the six of us together for years to come.

"Hey, Babe, you almost ready?" I called out to Brad as he primped in the bathroom getting dressed for dinner.

"Yeah, I'll be right out." By this time we had our routine down and every night we stopped off at the Acqua Pazza for a drink before dining. Sometimes the other guys would join us and sometimes not. The ship had pulled out from the harbor in Acapulco about two hours earlier so we were well out to sea.

We always enjoyed the piano music in the lounge before dinner and by this time had gotten to know our piano player Joel pretty well. We had ordered our drinks and it looked as though we would not be joined by either of the other two couples this evening. It was just Brad and me tonight. My cosmo and Brad's gin and tonic arrived and we sipped on them for maybe twenty minutes before it happened.

We felt the ship surge forward with a rumbling sound and then slow down. We all looked at one another and Joel started playing "The Morning After," the love theme from the Poseidon Adventure. It didn't occur to Brad or me that there could be a real problem with the ship. Then we heard the familiar seven short and one long emergency horn blasts. It still didn't register with us that there could be anything wrong and Joel kept playing the piano.

Suddenly, we noticed people were rushing from the dining room into the hallway. Then we began to get concerned. Just about that time a crew member came into the bar and announced, "People, this is not a drill or false alarm. Please, get your life jackets on and report to your lifeboat station immediately."

We rushed out of the bar but when I turned around, Brad wasn't behind me. I began to worry. Where had he gone? It wasn't long before he caught up to me. "Where were you?"

"I didn't want to leave without paying for our drinks." Such an honest man Brad is.

"The damn ship is going down and you're concerned with paying the bill?"

"Just don't worry about it. Where'd you put our life jackets?" Brad asked with a tone of panic in his voice.

"I stuffed them under the bed. I never thought we'd actually have to use them."

We started making our way back to our cabin, using only the stairwells since the elevators were shut down. Suddenly the lights went out and only emergency lighting was left to dimly light our way.

As we got closer to our cabin, I could smell smoke coming from the vents in the hallway. Entering our room, it was pitch dark inside. I got on the floor and started to feel under the bed for our life jackets.

"Here, Brad." I handed him a life jacket and then put mine on as well. "Is there anything else we need to take with us? Maybe the rest of that bottle of vodka?" I said half joking.

"No, c'mon -- let's just go."

I grabbed my iPhone since I would be lost without it even though I had no cellular service at sea. All my contacts are in that phone.

We got to our lifeboat station and the two crew attendants assigned to our area were already calling roll to make sure everyone was accounted for. We gave our names to be checked off the list and then began the long, long wait to see if we needed to evacuate the ship. The minutes turned into hours. We sang songs to entertain ourselves and some people had brought booze bottles that they passed around. The passengers were all being very patient but were concerned there may be more serious complications than were being revealed. Our two crew attendants were good about trying to keep us calm and apologized for this interruption to our evening.

Our lifeboat crew attendants had communication devices and we observed them talking several times with someone else regarding the conditions. I felt very safe for the most part -- just very tired and hungry. It was nearing ten o'clock, and we'd had no dinner. Once the distress signal went out over the radio waves, there were two other ships in the vicinity that stopped nearby and waited for us just in case they had to retrieve us from the ocean.

"Can I have your attention ...please? Quiet everyone! ...Shh!" A crew guy was trying to get our attention. "I want to caution everyone if we cannot lower the lifeboats in time and we are forced to jump overboard, please be sure to cross your arms over the top of your Mae West life vest. If you fail to do this, the impact with the water could cause the vest to snap your neck." Okay, that gave me cause for concern and now I was worried too. This announcement brought a hush over the group as we all contemplated an actual emergency evacuation.

Finally at about midnight, it was announced that we would be allowed to go into the Cabaret Lounge area and any of the other common areas but not back to our rooms. The power was still limited to emergency only but the danger of a major disaster had now passed.

Brad and I hoped to find John and Craig and Randy and Kevin and we wondered how Jack with Bruce fared in the mayhem. We staked out a place on the steps of the stage in the Cabaret Lounge and waited to see what would happen next. There was no PA system working so the staff tried to keep us entertained a capella. They announced that for those who were hungry, they'd soon be bringing out cake and juice and milk. They'd already distributed bottles of water.

As time passed we began to hear horror stories of the restrooms being backed up since there was no flushing capability. We enjoyed the attempt the crew made to keep us entertained and we made some new friendships talking with the people around us, but this was really getting old fast.

Finally, the lights flickered and came on and we could hear the engines begin to run again and everyone cheered. The Captain's voice came over the PA system.

"Ladies and Gentlemen, you are free to return to your cabins as we are out of danger at this time. I intend to assess the situation and damage caused by a fire in our engine room and I'll give you an update in the morning. If you don't wish to call it a night, our disco and all the main bars will be open serving free drinks all night. Please accept my apologies for this inconvenience and I'll give you an update soon."

It was a relief to finally feel like we could move about and go back to our cabin if we wanted to. It was after midnight but we were wide awake so we thought we'd drop off our life vests and head up to the dicso lounge for a free drink and maybe some dancing.

We were headed down the hall away from our cabin when suddenly we heard a loud scream followed by more screams and gasps.

"Now what?" I looked over at Brad and the two of us began to move swiftly in the direction of the main atrium lobby. Our floor was one of the mezzanine floors that overlooked the atrium. We looked down at the mass confusion on the floor below and still were not sure what the hysteria was about. There were several others now gathered, looking over the railing down onto the floor. I asked a guy next to us, "Do you know what's going on? What's all the hysteria about?"

He was pale like he'd seen a ghost and then he said, "Look at the water tube. Don't you see that?"

There it was, in the midst of the bubbles floating in the lower third of the beautiful seven-story glass tube of water, colorful lights shining on it – the dead body of a naked man.

9

Murder or Not

"I want to get closer and see if I can identify the body." The Private Investigator in me was coming out. I was curious. From where we were I could only tell that it appeared to be a young man of slight frame.

"There's no way I'm going down there with all that chaos." Brad was adamant about this. "You go ahead; I'll head up to the disco and meet you there when you're done."

I made my way down to the first floor of the atrium where the body seemed to be floating up and down in the water tube between the first and third floors. Curious on-lookers were crowding the floor but I managed to get close enough to get a better look at the corpse. There among the water bubbles, with a kaleidoscope of colored lights shining on his pallid body, I recognized him. I felt nauseous when I realized it was Jayde.

My first thoughts were of Bill -- wondering if someone had located him yet to give him the bad news. I felt sorry for him, regardless of the bizarre relationship he and Jayde appeared to have.

There wasn't much I could do here except to be in the way, so I decided to make my way up to the disco lounge. There I found Brad at a table with John and Craig and Randy and Kevin. They were all sharing details of their experience during the disaster and they'd heard the news of the body in the atrium water feature.

"Hey! You guys won't believe it. I'm so upset but it's good to see you guys," my voice still trembling.

"What is it, Hon? I'm glad you're here now. Tell us -- what did you discover?" Brad's words were comforting to me.

"So you guys are all fine? You survived the disaster?" I asked.

"Yeah, just a little hungry after all that time with no food." John was the first to speak up.

"Thankfully, Randy took his insulin with him and could monitor his diabetes while we waited to see what was going to happen."

Brad had moved over for me to sit next to him and asked, "So tell us Hon, did you get a look at the body? Do you know who it is?"

My stomach turned again as I recalled the image of Jayde floating in that water tube. "Yes, Brad, I did. It's Jayde."

"Oh my God …how awful. I wonder if anyone has told Bill yet?"

"I don't know. I didn't want to hang around there and

be in the way."

"So who's this Jayde guy? Do we know him?" Craig was curious to know.

"Remember, he was the one we told you about who was at our first dining table, the one who fought with his sugar daddy boyfriend. We pointed him out to you on the beach in Puerto Vallarta."

"Oh yea, I remember. I bit of a weird, freaky type."

We were all so hyped up from the events of the evening and at the thought of a possible murderer being on the ship that we couldn't consider going to bed. Randy and Kevin were first to turn in and try to get some sleep at about three in the morning but the rest of us stayed up until sunrise. I hadn't done that since my college days.

At about six thirty Brad and I returned to our suite to try and get a few hours of sleep. We'd only been down for about an hour and just dozed off when we were aroused by a knock at the door.

I stumbled to the door in the semi-darkness of the room in my boxer shorts.

"Mr. Felice?"

"Yes, I'm Tony Felice."

"Sorry to bother you at this time of the morning. I'm the ship's head Purser, Kyle Gardner. Captain Stubing requests to speak with you. I can escort you to the bridge if you like."

"Sure I guess. ...Just let me get dressed and I'll be right out."

"Very well, I'll wait for you here in the hall."

Rolling over in bed Brad said, "What's going on? What do they want?"

"I don't know. You go back to sleep and I should be back soon."

"You want me to go with you?"

"No, I'll be fine. I don't think I'm being arrested or anything. Get some sleep, Babe."

I reconnected with Mr. Gardner in the hallway and he escorted me to the bridge where Captain Stubing was waiting for me.

"Ah, Mr. Felice. Thank you for meeting with me at such an early hour of the day."

'Like I had a choice,' I thought to myself. He extended his hand to shake and introduced himself to me.

"I'm sure you're wondering what it is that I've called you here for."

"Well, yes sir, that thought had crossed my mind a time or two on the way over here."

"By now you're probably aware that a body was found on the ship late last night."

"Yes sir, I witnessed the body floating in the water tube."

"Terrible, terrible thing and the corporate owners of the *Serendipity of the Seas* would like to solve this mystery and get it put behind us with as little publicity as possible. You understand?"

"Yes sir, I do."

"In reviewing the ships roster, I see in your profile that you're the CEO of Balboa Investigating Agency?"

"Yes sir, I am." It felt good to say that.

"We here of the *Serendipity of the Seas* would like to hire you to investigate the death of this young man. We don't know if this was a terrible accident or if it was murder."

"Forgive me, sir, but I'm not so sure this was an accident -- but again, that is why you've come to me, correct?"

"Exactly, Mr. Felice."

"As long as you can assure me you'll give me full cooperation with your crew in the course of my investigation, I'd be glad to take on the case. Do we need to discuss my fee?"

"Mr. Felice, if you can solve this mystery, and do it quickly, your fee is of no concern to the corporate owners."

"Great, then let's get started."

"Very well. You tell me what you need from me." The Captain was being very cooperative.

"I'd like to look at the body for any evidence I can find and possible signs of the cause of death. I assume you have the body refrigerated somewhere on the ship?"

"That's correct. I can have one of my crew take you there now if you like."

I thought I should go back to our stateroom and let Brad know what was going on since I was sure he was curious why I was summoned to speak to the Captain. "I have a couple of things to take care of and then I can meet someone at ten o'clock this morning at the dining room. Will that work for you?"

"Perfect. I'll make sure Purser Gardner meets you there at ten."

When I got back to our stateroom, Brad was in the shower. I poured myself a cup of coffee that he'd ordered up for the room and took a chair out on the balcony. I wanted to begin to gather my thoughts and figure how I should approach this investigation.

Brad was cynical about me taking on this assignment, apparently feeling it would take away from our vacation time. I felt I needed to do my part and take on this challenge. Our vacation plans had already been altered greatly.

We were in the midst of a rather lively, heated discussion when the Captain's voice came over the PA system.

"Ladies and Gentlemen, this is your Captain speaking. I want to give you an update on the status of the Serendipity of the Seas *after last night's fire. As you have probably observed this morning, we're currently adrift and not moving. The fire last night in the engine room disabled three of the four engines that propel the ship. We have engineers being flown onto the ship by helicopter who can hopefully get at least two of the engines working again. Once that's accomplished, we will be heading back to port in Acapulco. Unfortunately*

we'll not be able to proceed with this cruise as it was planned. I'm sorry for the inconvenience and there'll, of course, be adjustments made to compensate you. I'll keep you updated as I get more information."

10

Foul Play

At ten o'clock I met up with Purser Kyle Gardner at the doors to the main dining room and he escorted me to the walk-in refrigeration box. I'd brought some plastic gloves and plastic collection bags for any evidence I might find. Since the body had been submerged in water for such a long time I doubted I'd find much.

Jayde's body was encased in a body bag and the initial shock of seeing his placid body once the bag was unzipped caused a flush to come over me, as well as a brief wave of nausea. It was something I've dealt with over and over when viewing a dead victim whenever the body is initially revealed to me. Luckily it's a feeling that always passes quickly so I can get in and do the job that I came to do.

From the bruises around Jayde's neck, it appeared obvious that he was strangled and the cause of death likely was asphyxiation. I noticed a few other minor scratches on his torso but nothing to indicate there was a murder object involved other than someone's bare hands. I took out my iPhone and snapped a few pictures of the marks on his body.

In checking his hands, I noticed one broken nail and what appeared to be skin under his fingernails. This was DNA and very important in the investigation, even though I had no way of having that DNA tested here at sea. I scrapped what substance I could find from under his nails and bagged it. The signs indicated there was a struggle before he died. There wasn't much more that I could find to aid in my investigation, but this was a start.

I had a hunch where I might find Brad -- having breakfast at the poolside café that the two of us frequented. I was hungry after the long restless night we'd had with little to eat, and I wanted to try and make amends with Brad, hoping he would understand the necessity of my taking on this investigation. Since our intended cruise had been disrupted anyway, I felt we could always take another cruise some other time.

After connecting for breakfast, Brad and I sat around the pool and watched the horizon bobbing up and down as we floated adrift at sea. Brad began to ask me questions about Jayde's death and started to show some interest in my investigation which made me feel much better. I always enjoy sharing my life and my passion with my man, and his suggestions couldn't hurt either.

Currently I'd nothing except that I was sure Jayde's death was not accidental. But the when and why and who were still questions to be answered.

The only access to the water feature was from the indoor pool level through a service closet door. It's conceivable that Jayde was murdered right there in the service closet after a struggle that ended in his death. But why was he nude? Could he have been murdered somewhere else and his body brought there and dumped? Possibly it was some sort of statement someone was making by stripping him and then humiliating his memory by throwing his nude body into the water feature where everyone could see him? Maybe someone had a grudge or vendetta?

Since the ship had been under a possible emergency evacuation and everyone was supposed to be at their lifeboat station, it was easier to speculate about when he was murdered. That entire emergency incident had taken several hours -- which gave plenty of time for a murder to take place with no witnesses. From the looks of the body when I first observed him floating in the tube of water, Jayde had already been in there for several hours. Therefore, it was most likely the murder had taken place when we were all out on deck waiting for clearance to return to the interior of the ship.

"So have you talked to Bill yet?" Brad was curious about my plans.

"Not yet but I do want to talk to him soon. He may know of someone who might have wanted Jayde killed. Maybe even someone who he may have upset here on the ship."

"What about that guy on the Blue Chairs Beach that Jayde got into an altercation with?"

"That's a good question, Brad. I hadn't thought about him, but then I'm not sure if he's even a passenger on our ship. Not sure if I would recognize him again if I came across him, but I'll keep that in mind. Thanks, Brad."

I spoke with Bill on the phone in his stateroom, offering my condolences and letting him know I was investigating Jayde's death for the cruise line. He agreed to meet with me later in the afternoon at the Acqua Pazza, before the dinner crowd started to file in and before Joel started playing.

Bill was already at a table in the bar with a cocktail as I walked up to him. I extended my hand to greet him and offer my sympathy, but he pulled me in for a hug.

"Again, Bill, let me say how sorry I am for your loss."

"I recognize you now. You were one of the guys that sat at our dining table the first night of the cruise."

"Exactly, wasn't sure you recognized the name when we talked on the phone earlier."

"I didn't then but I don't forget a face. What happened to you guys? You never came back." Bill seemed disappointed that we'd moved to another table for dining.

"Well, it's a long story but we hooked up with some friends that we knew prior to the cruise." I didn't have the heart to tell him the real reason we moved from his table. "How are you doing, Bill?"

"I'm okay. I just never dreamed that Jayde would be the first one to go, since I'm an old man and don't have that many more years. Jayde is …was so young."

"We just never know, do we? Bill, do you know of anyone on the ship who might have disliked Jayde enough to kill him?"

"No … no one that I know of. Everyone seemed to like him. He was a little quirky and weird but I loved him and most people did when they got to know him. … Do you really think he was murdered?"

I seemed to be getting nowhere. "Sadly, from all indications, he was murdered. …So there was no one that he fought with or didn't get along with? Maybe someone who was jealous of him? Anything at all that might lead us to a murderer?"

Bill was quiet, looking away.

"What is it, Bill? What's on your mind? You look like you have something you want to tell me."

"Well, there is something …but it's probably nothing."

"Let me be the judge of that, Bill. Just tell me what it is."

"It was like the second night of the cruise, and Jayde and I were leaving the disco. Actually we were asked to leave by the bouncer since Jayde had gotten into it with a couple of guys."

"What was he doing that caused you to get kicked out?"

"Just his usual behavior. He was flirting and playing with some guy at the bar which was no surprise to me. This guy's boyfriend got ticked off and wanted to pick a fight with Jayde. So we were asked to leave."

"I see." I was curious now. "Go on, Bill. What happened next?"

"Well, as we were leaving we took the elevator and when we stepped in, this guy stepped in behind us. He shut off the elevator and pinned Jayde against the wall. He was mad as hell, and threatened Jayde."

"What did he say?"

"I don't remember his exact words but it was something to the effect *'If I ever catch you fucking with by man, I'll kill you, bastard.'*"

"Wow! And did you report this incident?"

"No, I just took it as an idle threat …but do you think this guy may have actually killed Jayde?"

"It's possible, Bill. I'll want to question him. Do you know his name by chance?"

"No, I never really talked to him, but I can tell you he would not be hard to locate. He's a big muscle dude, sort of like the Mr. Clean man with a shaved head. He always wears tank tops around the ship showing off a major-size tattoo on his right shoulder. It's like a big dragon in colors of blue and green with a little orange as well. Oh, and he has a goatee also. He's very easy to recognize and a bit intimidating."

"Thanks, Bill, I'll try to locate him and question him about this incident and his threat. Now, what about that night when Jayde died? We'd all been evacuated. Was he at the lifeboat station with you and the rest of the passengers?"

Bill looked a little puzzled but replied, "Yes, of course, we were both there like everyone else. Why do you ask?"

"Just trying to narrow down a timeline to determine when Jayde might have been murdered. ...I think that's all I have for you now and if you think of anything else that might be of help to me, here's my business card. I've written my cabin number on the back for you. Give me a call in my room, any time."

"I'll do that. And, Tony, please find whoever did this to my boy, Jayde. I'll miss him," Bill pleaded with me.

"I'll do my best, Bill. You can be sure of that."

Early the next morning we awoke to the sound of a helicopter circling over the ship. The upper rear recreation deck doubled as a heliport in emergencies. Hopefully, these were the engineers coming in to work on the disabled ship's engines to get us back to Acapulco.

Brad and I were headed out to the pool café to grab

some breakfast when the Captain's voice came over the PA system.

"Ladies and gentlemen, this is your Captain speaking. I want to give you an update on our engine room problems and the projected itinerary for the Serendipity *of the Seas. You may have heard the helicopter this morning that landed on the ship with engineers who will be working to get the damaged engines running again. Once that's done, we can head back to port at Acapulco. You'll hear from me again when I've more information for you. Until then, enjoy a day by the pool where all day today the cocktails at the pool bar are complimentary. Again I apologize for the inconvenience, and appreciate your cooperation."*

11

Closing in on a Suspect

Brad and I enjoyed some time at the pool with John and Craig and later Randy and Kevin who joined us. As much as I tried to get my mind off the investigation, I couldn't help but think about Jayde and wonder who could have strangled him. We listened to the Reggae sounds of the steel pan band poolside and had our share of free drinks. Fortunately, the alcohol content was minimal, keeping us from becoming too intoxicated. It was still nice to order a drink and not have to pay for it, a nice gesture on the part of the Captain.

I excused myself at about three o'clock to go speak with the Captain regarding an idea I had. I was glad that the boys didn't question me much on the investigation details or what thoughts I had on the case.

∾

"Excuse me, sir can I speak with you for a minute?" I was at the door to the bridge and Captain's office where I was met by a security guard.

"Yes, yes, please do come in. …It's alright, Hans."

"Sorry to bother you, Captain, but I have a request."

"Not a problem, Tony. Anything you need. I want to help in whatever way I can."

"I'd like to locate a picture of Jayde from the ship's photographer and publish it in the daily bulletin that goes out to all the rooms and ask for anyone with information to contact me. Do you think we can do that? Is that all right?"

"Of course! Not a problem. You think maybe someone might have seen something?"

"I don't know but it's worth a try. Right now most of the passengers only know that someone died on the ship, and most likely was murdered, but they aren't able to put a face with the individual."

"I'll call the photo shop and let them know you'll be stopping by and they'll cooperate with you to get what you need from them. Then you can see Purser Gardner at his desk and give him the information you want printed in the bulletin. We should be able to have that for tomorrow's publication."

"Thanks, Captain, that'll be great. I'll go down to the photo shop right now."

It was pretty easy to locate a usable picture of Jayde.

The ship's photographer seemed to know right away who I was talking about from my description of Jayde. I put together a quick write-up to publish with the picture asking anyone with any information to contact me at my stateroom or contact the Captain. Hopefully someone saw something that night that would help in my investigation.

The next morning we awoke to the sounds of the ship engines and could feel that we were moving once again. It was still very early, just after day break, so we felt sure we would be hearing an update from the Captain soon.

As I stumbled in the dim light to the bathroom, I noticed the daily bulletin that had been slid under the door sometime in the pre-dawn hours. I was anxious to see how my request looked and was hoping it might bring some new information.

"Look, Brad, here's the notice I put in the bulletin. It looks good and that's a nice picture of Jayde."

Brad was anxious to read the notice. "That turned out well, Hon, and I'm sure if anyone has information, this will bring them forward."

"I sure hope so. I don't have a lot to go on right now."

A few hours later, before heading down to breakfast, the Captain addressed the passengers again with an update.

"Ladies and Gentlemen, this is your Captain speaking. You probably have already noticed that the Serendipity of the Seas *is sailing once again. We've managed to get two of the engines running and are headed back in a northerly direction. Instead of returning to Acapulco, I've decided to take the ship all the way back to San Diego. Moving at a slower speed it could take three days or more to get back.*

"Many of you have been asking what sort of compensation the cruise company plans to offer its passengers. I'm pleased to announce that I'm authorized to inform you the Serendipity of the Seas *is offering a full refund or a future booking of your choice on any of our ship's itineraries. More information will follow on how to handle your adjustment. We should have smooth seas and plenty of sun for the trip home so relax and enjoy the time aboard the ship."*

෴

After breakfast I told Brad I wanted to locate "Mr. Clean" and find out his side of the story. I needed to get his name too and check his whereabouts during the emergency …see if he had an alibi. Right now he was my only lead.

It occurred to me, since Bill had told me the guy was a muscle dude, I could likely find him some time during the day along with his boyfriend working out in the gym. I stopped off at the gym and poked my head inside but there was only a small framed guy on a treadmill, watching some sort of nature video. I decided to find a lounge chair on the deck near the gym entrance and hang out for a while in the hopes "Mr. Clean" might show.

It wasn't long, maybe thirty minutes, before the two muscle dudes came struttin' towards the gym door. I could spot "Mr. Clean" easily, just as Bill had said. His tattoo was very prominent and he was really buffed, just like he described him. He also appeared to be very arrogant.

Approaching him as he set up the bench press I said, "Excuse me, I'm Private Investigator Felice investigating the case of the murdered young man on the ship. Can I have a few minutes to ask you some questions?"

"What for? I don't know nuttin." He seemed defensive but I managed to get him to step outside on the deck where we had privacy to talk.

I showed him a picture of Jayde. "You were implicated in an altercation that you had with this young man and I wanted to hear what you have to say about the incident." This guy seemed like a real jarhead with not a lot going for him in the way of personality.

"So, whadda you wanna know?"

"First off, can I get your name?"

"Mike! That's all, just Mike. That's all you need to know."

"Okay, Mike, do you recognize this guy, the one who was found dead?" I showed him the picture again of Jayde.

"Yeah, I seen him around."

"Do you remember having some words with him and threatening him in the elevator when you guys were asked to leave the disco lounge one evening?"

"Sure! The asshole white trailer trash was fucking with my man and I didn't appreciate it."

"Did you threaten to kill him?"

"Yeah, so what of it? I didn't really mean I was actually going to kill him. I just wanted to scare the shithead and make sure he stayed away from my property, my man …you know?"

"So, Mike, on the night of the disaster can you verify for me where you were at the time the emergency alarm sounded?"

"Of course. I was at my lifeboat station like everyone else. You can verify that with the crew."

About that time his boyfriend poked his head outside from the gym to see if everything was all right.

"Thanks, Mike. I'll be checking out your story and might have more questions for you later."

"Hey, no problem. I ain't got nuttin to hide. The kid was an asshole but he didn't need to die."

∽

We were just about to leave our stateroom for lunch when there was a knock at the door. It was Purser

Gardner. "Mr. Felice, the Captain has sent me to escort you to the bridge. Seems you have a response to the notice we published overnight in the ship's bulletin."

"Great. Let me grab a note pad. I'll be right with you." Stepping back inside our room, I kissed Brad and told him I'd hook up with him later, likely at the pool.

"Good luck, Hon. Hope this provides some information for you."

"Thanks, Babe!"

As I walked into the bridge control room, I noticed that the Captain was in his office sitting at his desk talking with a young man.

"Good afternoon, Tony. This is Scott."

I extended my hand to shake as Scott stood to greet me.

The Captain began, "Scott read your notice in the bulletin this morning and immediately recognized Jayde's picture. He has some information that may or may not be helpful to you."

"Great. Thanks for coming forward, Scott. So tell me how it is that you recognize Jayde."

Scott seemed a little nervous but he took a deep breath and began to tell his story. "Well, it was the evening of the disaster, something like seven o'clock maybe. Several of us guys were at the indoor pool and spa. There were only a few guys in there at that time of the evening."

"And that is where you met Jayde?"

"I actually never really met him. As I say, several of us were in the pool and then decided to go into the spa. Once we got into the spa, the swimsuits came off."

"So Jayde was one of the guys in the spa with you?" Knowing Jayde I could pretty much imagine what happened next.

"Yes. We all started talking -- you know some trash talk. Then we started with some groping -- just having some fun, right?"

"I know how that goes. And so what happened?"

"Well, Jayde was pretty horny. He sat on the edge of the spa with this raging hard-on. We were all enjoying his playfulness and showing off for us."

"Did Jayde have anyone else there at the pool who appeared to be his boyfriend or partner?"

"No, not that I could tell. I felt sure he was single. ...Did he have a partner on the ship?" Scott appeared puzzled.

"Yes, Scott, an older gentleman, much older, named Bill. So go on with your story."

"Well, as I said, Jayde was sitting on the edge of the spa with his hard cock and one of the crew from the ship came out and headed over towards the spa. Apparently he was headed to service that water thing in the atrium area."

The Captain spoke up. "Yes, we have a crewman who takes care of cleaning and servicing the water tube every other day. I think he'd have been scheduled to service it the evening of the disaster."

"Well," said Scott, "this guy walked over towards the spa like I said and once he noticed Jayde was totally erect, he just stared as he walked slowly by. He couldn't take his eyes off of his cock and, of course, Jayde enjoyed this."

"So did this guy stick around ...and what did Jayde do?"

"The guy went through a concealed access door that apparently went out to the water tube. He left the door slightly ajar which Jayde apparently took to be a come-on. He wasted no time in grabbing his towel and headed out through this door and we never saw him again."

"About how long was it then from that time until the disaster warning sounded on the ship for passengers to report to the lifeboat station?"

"That was maybe fifteen minutes or so later, but we never saw Jayde after he left the spa. We grabbed our suits and towels and headed out."

"What did the crew guy look like who Jayde followed? Is there anything else you can tell me about Jayde and that evening?"

"There isn't anything else that I can think of. The guy who was with the crew was attractive, probably in his 40's, with an olive complexion and salt and pepper hair. I noticed this because I thought he was attractive too and is my type. Do you think he could have murdered Jayde?"

"I don't know, Scott, but this is some very helpful information. I'm going to do my best to find out who killed Jayde. If you should think of anything else that might help me, here's my card with my stateroom number on the back. You can call me direct any time."

Scott left the bridge and I was feeling good about the information he was able to provide. I immediately turned to the Captain. "So, do you have the name of your crew member who was servicing the water tube that evening? I think he sounds like my number one suspect."

"His name is Humberto. He's been with this ship for maybe four years now, a resident of Brazil. I'll arrange to have him meet with the two of us and will let you know when that's set up."

"Thanks, Captain."

12

Puzzle Pieces

We decided to order breakfast in our stateroom and enjoy a relaxing morning together on the balcony. A rich, bold cup of café au lait, buttery croissants and fresh fruit compote with yogurt topping, this was a very relaxing way to start the day and enjoyable being with Brad in such a peaceful setting.

"You know, Babe, there's something that doesn't make sense to me." I was bothered by a thought that had come to me in bed earlier.

"What's that?"

"Well, Scott said that Jayde disappeared with this guy from the ship just before the emergency alarm went off, maybe 15 minutes."

"Yeah ...so?"

"Well, when I spoke with Bill, he said that Jayde was with him at the lifeboat station during the disaster."

"Doesn't sound possible, does it?"

"Yeah, that's what I'm thinking. I can probably verify that pretty easily with the roster checklist taken at the lifeboat station. Remember our lifeboat attendant took a roll call of everybody present?"

The phone rang in our room and it was the Captain. He wanted to let me know he'd arranged to have Humberto meet the two of us on the bridge at two o'clock, where we could talk with him in the Captain's office.

Later that morning I went to speak with Captain Stubing. I was curious to know about Jayde's whereabouts during the disaster. He called Crystal up to the bridge to speak with us. Crystal was the attendant in charge of the lifeboat station where Bill and Jayde were assigned. The Captain had already pulled up the roster on his computer for that evening and told me that Jayde was not checked in. We both just wanted to double check with Crystal and see if she could shed any light on any other details. She was emphatic that Jayde did not check in even though she had called his name several times during the long ordeal waiting for the Captain to give clearance to return to the interior of the ship. She did recall Bill being present but not Jayde.

Was Bill hiding something? Why would he not know that Jayde wasn't there on the deck at the lifeboat station? Was he covering for someone?

∾

It was right at two o'clock when I approached the door to the bridge and was met by a security guard. He brought me over to the Captain's office where Humberto was already seated and talking with the Captain.

"Tony, come in, please. This is Humberto, one of my crew members aboard the ship."

Humberto stood and I shook his hand. "I'm Tony Felice, a private investigator."

"Detective Particular." The Captain responded to the puzzled look on Humberto's face. "Tony, Humberto understands a lot of English but prefers to speak in Portuguese, the language of his native country, Brazil. I can translate his response but I think for the most part, he'll understand your questions."

This could be a challenge but thankfully the Captain spoke Portuguese fluently. "Nice to meet you, Humberto. I have a few questions for you and I want you to just relax and not be nervous."

He seemed to be fidgety and uncomfortable, but when the boss calls you to his office to speak to a private investigator, anyone would likely be nervous.

I showed a picture of Jayde to Humberto. "Do you recognize this man?"

"Sim, eu conheço ele." "He said he knows who that is."

"When did you first meet this man?"

"Foi na noite do incendio." "He said it was the night of the disaster aboard the ship."

"Where was it that you first saw him or actually met him?"

"*Eu vi ele com outros caras nus na piscina.*" "He said he first saw him naked in the swimming pool area."

"And what were you doing at that time in the pool area?"

"*Eu estava trabalhando. Eu mantenho o tubo de agua naquela hora.*" "He said he was working – that's the time of day he usually services the water feature. That's true -- he usually does service the water tube at that time several days a week."

"So then how was it that you met this young man?"

There was a long pause as Humberto thought about his answer. "*Ele me seguiu ate dentro do gabinete de serviço. Ele so estava usando uma toalha. Me fez ficar nervoso.*" "He said Jayde followed him to the service closet wearing only a towel and that made him uncomfortable."

"So then what happened?"

"*Nada. Eu sai quando ouvi o alarme de emergencia.*" "He says he left once he heard the emergency alarm sound."

"The alarm didn't go off for a while after you made the connection with this man. In that time did you have any sexual relations with him?"

Humberto looked puzzled. The Captain translated for him and then he responded. "*Não, não, eu fiquei com medo e não queria ser pego e perder meu emprego. Eu deixei ele assim que ouvi o alarme soar.*" "He says absolutely not -- he was afraid he might get caught with this guy and lose his job. He said he left as soon as he heard the emergency alarm sound."

It was still puzzling to me what went on during the time Humberto was with Jayde. Was he not telling the truth about not having a sexual encounter and could he be telling other lies as well? It was starting to sound like nothing really happened after all between these two unless he was afraid to tell me the truth in front of the Captain.

"So when you left this man, was there anyone else there with him or with the two of you?"

"Não. Eu não vi ninguem. Eu so queria sair de la." "He says he didn't see anyone else and just wanted to get out of there."

"And when you left, Humberto, where did you go?"

"Eu fui para a estação de salva-vidas para a tripulação, como me ensinaram." "He said he went to his lifeboat station as he'd been instructed. Let me check the crew roster to see if he was checked in that night."

The Captain turned to his computer and pulled up the list from the check-ins that night at the lifeboat station. "He's correct. He was accounted for that evening."

I turned to the Captain, "Well unless you have anything further for Humberto, I think I'm satisfied with questioning for now."

I could see that Humberto wasn't quite getting all that I was saying but once the Captain translated for him, he smiled and nodded. *"Obrigado."* "Thank you, too, Humberto. If we have anything else for you, the Captain will contact you."

Humberto left the office and I felt like I still had nothing to go on. I believed he was telling the truth and hadn't had sex with Jayde. My first thought was maybe Humberto got mad because Jayde had tempted him into doing something sexual. I could see him struggling with Jayde and accidentally in a rage killing him. That, however, didn't seem to be the case based on what I'd just heard.

"Well, Captain, still not much to go on. I have a request, however. ...Is there a way for you to drain the water from the water feature?"

"Yes, of course, I can do that. We need to drain it anyway since Jayde was floating dead in there for so long."

"Great, so it will be completely empty? And then can I somehow get down to the bottom once it's empty? I'm looking for any evidence there might be -- although I'm not expecting anything."

"Yes, Tony, we have a rope ladder that we use to get down to the bottom once the glass tube is empty. I'll have someone start pumping the water out to sea right away. It will take several hours because it pumps slowly and that's a lot of water. It should be ready for you tomorrow morning."

"Thanks, Captain, I'll check back with you in the morning."

I headed back to our stateroom hoping that Brad

would be there so I could tell him about the conversation with Humberto. I always liked getting Brad's perspective on things since he had such good insight into people.

Brad wasn't there but I figured I could likely find him at the pool. It was only a matter of minutes before I heard the door open and Brad walked in.

"Hey, Hon, you'll never guess who I just saw," Brad seemed excited to tell me.

"Okay, who did you see?"

"That guy in Puerto Vallarta who was involved in the altercation with Jayde on the beach."

"Wow, so he is on this ship? Where did you see him?" I was excited that Brad had identified him.

"He was laying out at the pool."

"Do you think he's still there?"

"I'd imagine so. I just saw him and he didn't seem like he was leaving any time soon."

I jumped up and gathered my note pad, and Brad and I went out to the pool so that Brad could point him out to me.

Once I saw him again I recognized him and Brad let me approach him on my own.

"Excuse me, how are you?"

The guy had earbuds in listening to his iTunes and could barely hear me. He looked at me standing there and removed his earbuds. "Did you say something?"

"Yes, I'm Tony Felice and I'm a PI investigating a case

aboard ship. I'd like to ask you some questions if you don't mind."

"Questions …about what?"

I handed him a picture of Jayde and asked if he recognized him. "Yeah, isn't this the dude that was found dead on the ship?"

"Correct! I recall earlier in the week while we were in Puerto Vallarta that you had some sort of altercation with this young man on the Blue Chairs beach. Can you tell me what that was about?"

"Yeah man, it was nothing, no big deal." He seemed reluctant to talk about the details.

"Just the same, I need to know what happened. And before we get started with that, can I get your full name for my notes?"

"Dude, I don't know you from Adam. Do you have some sort of ID or something? I don't like where this is going."

This guy seemed to be awfully defensive -- almost like he was guilty of something or hiding something from me. I showed him my detective badge and picture ID and I wrote down his name as he appeared to be more cooperative with me after verifying my identity.

"So what was the cause of the scuffle on the beach between you two?"

"Well …I guess there's no polite way to say this and I'm sure it's not your first time hearing this. This dude approached me in the public men's room on the beach and offered me a blow job."

"So you took him up on his gracious offer?"

"Hell yeah! It didn't take long. This kid seemed to know what he was doing, like he'd done it many times before."

"So then what happened after you got off with him?"

"The damn shithead wanted me to pay him. That was never part of the deal. I started to ignore him and walk away and he tried to start a fight saying I stole money from him."

"Is that when the police showed up?"

"Yeah, and after they showed up this kid backed off and it all sort of went away. I didn't think anything more of it. The cops just blew off the whole thing."

"So did you have any desire to kill him? Were you holding a grudge from this incident?"

"Hell no. I'd forgotten all about it until you brought it up. It wasn't a big deal."

"Thanks for your cooperation and here's my card with my cabin number on the back. Please give me a call if you think of anything that might help me with my investigation."

"Sure, dude, good luck with that. The kid was a shithead but didn't deserve to die."

13

Putting the Puzzle Together

I wanted to speak to Bill but didn't want to give him a heads up before doing so. I was hoping to catch him off guard, and figured that if Brad and I went down to dinner early, we might catch Bill as he joined the line outside the dining room before the doors opened. We headed down to dinner at least thirty minutes early and found a cluster of lounge chairs outside the dining room where we could kick back and wait.

I kept watching the hallway and the elevators that accessed the main dining room floor level. Then, almost as though it were scripted, Bill stepped off the elevator and headed towards us. He was very conspicuous in full kilt paraphernalia. I walked up to greet him.

"Bill, how are you this evening? You're looking very dapper, I must say."

Bill was quick to let me know the kilt was a family tartan and even the sporran pouch bore a family crest. He seemed to be very proud of his Scottish heritage. "Thank you, Tony. I'm doing pretty well, under the circumstances."

We'd started to walk towards the dining room. "Bill, can we sit here and talk? I have a couple of things I want to ask you."

"Sure, no problem, we're too early for dinner yet anyway."

We located a couple of cocktail lounge chairs in the area where Brad was seated, but far enough away to allow for some privacy.

"Bill, the night of the disaster you told me that Jayde was with you at the lifeboat station. But according to the roster check-in at your station, Jayde was not accounted for."

Bill looked a little uncomfortable with my question. "Really? Well, I could have sworn he was there. I didn't mean to mislead you, but it's difficult for me to face the fact that I'm getting pretty forgetful in my old age, you know, and I'm so used to Jayde always being gone that sometimes I don't even realize whether he's there or not."

"So you admit that it's likely Jayde wasn't there and actually could have already been deceased at that time?"

"Yes, I guess so. ...Look, I don't really like talking about this stuff. I'm still in mourning and missing my boy, so if you'll excuse me, I'm going to my table." And with that comment, Bill got up and walked off.

That got me nowhere but at least it explained the discrepancy in the two stories about Jayde's whereabouts during the disaster -- which means he may have already been killed or was killed shortly after the emergency alarm sounded. But could I believe his "forgetfulness" story? Was he actually hiding something more from me?

I headed over to where Brad had been seated. He was already standing as I approached so the two of us could enter the dining room. "How did that go?"

"Not well at all. Bill cut short our conversation."

We were both looking forward to dinner and spending some time with our friends and dining mates.

I woke up at the first light of day, after a restless night. I kept thinking the cruise would be over soon and we'd be back at the pier in San Diego, and I didn't have much to go on with this murder. I was looking forward to getting down inside the water tube once it was drained in hopes there may be some evidence. I wasn't all that hopeful, however.

I did still have the DNA evidence I'd collected from under Jayde's fingernails that I could have analyzed when I got back home. But without a suspect to compare the DNA to, it might not be much help. I knew that the Captain really wanted to have this resolved before we docked and I really wanted to fulfill my commitment to him. Besides that, the money incentive from my fees should I be able to solve this case was a motivation for me too.

Heading to the bridge to see the Captain, I passed by the water tube and saw that it was empty. It was still early morning -- probably the best time for me to do my research, before too many people were out and moving around. I didn't like the idea of a lot of people watching me examine the inside of the glass tube for clues.

The Captain had a crew member escort me from the bridge to the service closet accessing the water tube. The young man attached a rope ladder and dropped it into the tube. Before he let me begin my descent, he tested it with his weight to make sure it was secure.

I made my way slowly to the bottom on the unstable rope ladder. As I began to search, there seemed to be nothing there, no evidence. Searching every inch of the floor surface and every crevasse, I still found nothing -- not even the broken fingernail that I noticed on Jayde when I inspected his body. If it had broken off in here, it had likely been pumped out to sea with the water.

I was just about to give up and call it quits when I felt the need to check the grate covering the drain in the center of the floor once more. As I looked into the side of the well under the grate, something shiny caught my eye. I took out my pocket knife and managed to pry the grate open. There it was, the evidence I had hoped to find. I was ecstatic and so glad I had searched the water tube. There in the corner, thankfully wedged so that it hadn't been dislodged by the water pumps, was a gold

Krugerrand -- just like the one Bill had been wearing on a chain around his neck the night we first met him at dinner. Thoughts were racing in my head as I climbed back up out of the water tube. I needed to talk with the Captain and the two of us needed to have a talk with Bill.

"Tony, come in. Please, come in." The Captain welcomed me to the bridge. "Any luck with your inspection of the water tube, Tony?"

"Actually, yes, I found something very interesting. Can you have someone locate Bill and bring him here so we can talk with him?"

I spent a few minutes discussing the new evidence I'd found and my suspicions with the Captain, while someone escorted Bill to the bridge. We decided to use the conference table to speak with Bill instead of the desk in the Captain's office. My intention was not to hold back with Bill since he'd been lying to me all along and I wanted him to tell me the truth.

"Bill, good morning. Won't you come in and have a seat?" I stood up as the Captain welcomed Bill to the table.

"Good morning, Captain. …Tony. So what's this about? Do you have some new information on Jayde's death?"

"Yes, you could say that." I decided to cut right to the chase and take a hard accusatory line of questioning with him. I tossed the plastic evidence bag containing the Krugerrand onto the table. "Do you recognize this?"

"Yes, my Krugerrand. Where did you find it? I was looking for that."

"I found it where you lost it, Bill."

"What do you mean?" Bill had a puzzled look.

"I found this in the bottom of the water tube. Any idea how it might have gotten there?"

"I don't know but I assume Jayde was wearing it the night he died. He borrowed my jewelry many times and must have worn it that night he was killed."

I wasn't buying his story. Jayde was not the bling type of guy unless it was for a piercing on his body. I stood up and walked around the table behind Bill who was leaning forward with his head bowed resting his forehead in his left hand.

I returned to my seat after making a complete lap around the table. "It's over, Bill. Give it up and tell us what really happened that night. I'm tired of your lies."

"What do you mean? I told you everything I know," Bill pleaded.

"Well, to start with, why don't you tell us how you got those scratches on your neck?" I had observed the red abrasions on his neck that were usually concealed by his starched oxford cloth shirts. Leaning over the table with his head down had made it possible for me to see them as I walked behind him.

"And if you'd roll up the sleeve on your right arm and show us the scratch there. ...Tell us how you got that one as well." I'd noticed the redness and welts on his arm not long after Jayde had died but hadn't made the connection at that time.

Bill now buried his head in both hands. He started to mumble something.

"Speak up, Bill. Tell us the whole story."

14

The Confession

"I was heartbroken. It was the ultimate betrayal. …I don't know why he would do this to me." Bill was almost in tears as he spoke.

"Do what to you, Bill? Tell us what you know and tell us how this happened."

"After all I had to offer him and after taking him in when he had no one. …NO ONE in his life that could take care of him like I could. I was there for him."

Bill seemed to be getting agitated but I tried to keep him calm so he could get his story out. "So just start from the beginning and tell us exactly what happened, Bill."

"Damn him. …We made plans for this cruise about nine months ago. We were both pretty excited. For a long time, Jayde was happy and always there for me as a companion and a lover.

"I know I'm an old man and Jayde was very sexual and needed more from me than I could deliver. I knew that and that was fine with me. I knew of his sexual exploits, but he seemed to always come home to me and I thought we were happy together. ...I was."

Bill paused. "Go ahead Bill. Talk it all out."

"About four months ago our relationship still felt pretty solid -- at least I thought it did. As time went by and it got closer to the cruise date, I was looking forward to a nice vacation with Jayde, sort of a second honeymoon. But all that changed before we left. ...Can I get a drink of water please?"

The Captain left the table and came back with a bottle of water for Bill.

I began to question Bill again after he appeared ready. "So you say things changed? How so? What changed, Bill?"

"It was probably two weeks before the cruise. I was home outside by the pool on one of the oversized lounge chairs with my back to the house. I was nearly asleep when I heard Jayde come in the front door into the living room. He was on his cell phone, so I didn't jump up to greet him. He was always talking on that damn phone with one of his many friends. He apparently didn't realize I was home and couldn't see me laying on the lounge. He was talking freely and loudly, not trying at all to hide his conversation.

"I usually play cards with my friends at the Community Center on that day and don't usually get home until much later. On this particular day I'd gone in to play cards with the guys but I had a miserable headache and so I came home early."

"So, Bill, what was it that you overheard Jayde talking about?"

Bill took a breath and started again. "I realized he was talking to someone that was more than just a friend. He called him sweetie several times and I could tell by the tone of his voice that this was a love interest. He was having an affair.

"He said... he said... Sorry... I heard him say just two more weeks and they could be together at last. It sounded obvious that he wanted out of our relationship."

Bill broke down and started to sob. "I'm so sorry, Bill." I offered my condolence.

"After Jayde got off the phone, I lay there on the lounge and pretended to be sound asleep. I didn't want him to know I'd heard the whole conversation. It worked. He bought it.

"Jayde had become so blatant with his sexual escapades that at times it was very embarrassing for me. I was really getting tired of the way he'd been treating me, and now this. But I still loved him and wanted him in my life and I realized I needed to be up front and tell him that I was bothered by his behavior. So I decided to go ahead and take the cruise with Jayde and try to convince him of my love for him and my financial means to support him. Jayde liked nice things but never wanted to work, so I thought that might convince him to change his behavior and not to leave. I know it was rather naïve of me to think he would actually change for me."

"So, Bill, what happened that led you to murder him after all. How did that happen?"

"I didn't murder Jayde! I could never do that. I loved him. Is that why I'm here? You think I murdered him? No… no. You've got that all wrong."

"Then why don't you tell us what happened, Bill."

"That night of the fire on the ship, Jayde and I had gone down to the pool area. I planned to just kick back and relax but Jayde had his swim suit on and planned to go in the pool. I was back a ways from the pool's edge in a quiet corner laying down relaxing. Jayde was in the pool with a group of guys he'd just befriended. The group of them headed over to the spa and I noticed the swimsuits came off and the boys were all getting pretty playful. That was no big deal to me -- I'd been there myself and I was used to that with Jayde by now."

"That still must have been difficult for you," I said.

"I was actually okay at first. Then Jayde was becoming very horny and was sitting on the edge of the spa with his beautiful hard cock being appreciated by everyone, and being played with by some as well. Then one of the crew came out to the pool and I wondered if he would try and stop the little orgy going on, but instead, he seemed to be mesmerized with Jayde and his erect dick. He stared and walked by the group orgy of guys slowly, not taking his eyes off of Jayde."

After a brief moment of silence, I asked, "How did that make you feel, Bill? Were you jealous of that?"

"I was fine at that point. I'd seen similar incidents unfold with Jayde before. But then the crew guy disappeared inside a concealed door behind the spa and Jayde immediately got up, wrapped a towel around him and followed this guy through the door. I watched for a while thinking he'd be coming right back out, but he didn't. My thoughts started to run away with me, wondering what was going on. Finally I couldn't take it any longer."

"So what did you do?" I asked.

"I got up and headed over to where the door was and managed to slip in to an area that I guess was used to service the water feature. I stayed quiet in the darkness and wasn't noticed by either Jayde or this other guy. They were in the middle of something and not paying much attention to what was going on around them."

I pretty much knew what was going on in there, but I had to ask. "Bill, what was it that they were doing?"

Bill was struggling now and took a deep breath and a drink of water. "This crew guy had his pants down and Jayde was giving him a blow job. I watched for a while and the rage was building inside me. I started thinking of how fed up I was with his sexual escapades. And then to overhear that he had a boyfriend, a secret sexual affair

that he planned to leave me for. I was furious with him.
But then the emergency alarm sounded.

"The crew guy pulled up his pants and left abruptly
and I approached Jayde right there near the water
feature. We began to argue and my rage elevated to the
point where I wanted to kill him. I started to strangle
him but he fought back for his life. He knew I'd had all
I could take. That was when he grabbed at the chain
around my neck. But suddenly, he lost his balance
and started falling backwards into the water tube. For
just a split second, I felt it was justice that he should be
found naked in that glass water tube after all the times
he'd been so promiscuous. But I couldn't let him die. I
realized my rage was out of control and I reached out
and saved him. The alarm was still blasting, and at that
point I figured I would be lucky if the ship went down
and we all perished with it."

My interest aroused, I asked, "So then what did you
do, Bill? You saved Jayde from falling into the water tube
and then what happened?"

"I walked out and left Jayde standing there naked. I
could never kill him, you gotta believe me. I loved him."
Bill was sobbing heavily now.

"Why, Bill? Why didn't you tell us this from the
beginning? Why lie to me about that evening?"

"I just felt like no one would believe me so it was best
if I denied to myself that our confrontation that night

ever happened."

I was still not convinced that Bill was telling me the whole truth but his body language and reactions to my questions seemed believable. If he didn't do it, that still left the question of who did kill Jayde. Who else was there that night after Bill left Jayde?

"So, Bill, did you report to your lifeboat station right away after leaving Jayde?"

"Yes. Yes I did."

"And did you see anyone else leaving the pool area when you left Jayde?"

"I don't recall seeing anyone but it was all very hectic with the emergency and all that was going on. I don't think there was anyone around."

This entire story, starting with the boyfriend and the telephone conversation, could have been made up by Bill. But this was all I could get out of him right now and, although I still had my doubts as to what actually happened that night, I would assume for the moment that he was telling the truth. Still having no real suspects and getting frustrated, I decided to spend the rest of the day with Brad and let my frustrations go for now.

15

A Breakthrough

It was the second to the last evening on the ship and I was looking forward to being with friends tonight. The six of us dining mates decided to make reservations at the Italian Restaurant on the ship and enjoy a quiet evening together.

We vowed to all keep in touch and get together at least twice a year either in Palm Springs or in San Diego. Brad and I always enjoyed any excuse to get away to Palm Springs, so keeping that commitment wouldn't be difficult for us.

After dinner we all went our own ways to enjoy the evening and figured we'd at some point all end up at the disco club for some cocktails and one last night of dancing. Brad and I strolled through the casino playing a few bills on the slots and watching the high rollers on the craps table. We saw Jack out enjoying his last night of gambling after putting Bruce in bed for the night.

We strolled down the hallway towards the gift

shops, window shopping at the Tiffany, Gucci and Louis Vuitton shops. I picked up a bottle of Gran Marnier to take home since the price was so good on the ship.

We then headed down to the photo gallery to see if there were any other photos we wanted to select before going home. There were a few taken of the group of us at dinner and then a few candid shots pool-side that we found. I was enjoying wandering thru the gallery checking out all the pictures of other passengers and was amazed at so many faces that I didn't recognize after spending so much time together on the ship. I noticed a section with a sign titled "Love Birds." That caught my eye and I wanted to see if Brad and I made the board without our knowing it.

I quickly scanned the pictures and recognized some of the subjects from the ship. Then suddenly, I was drawn to one picture in particular. It was of Jayde. He was in a passionate lip lock with a young strawberry blond guy. This was no one that I recognized, but maybe he had more than a casual connection with Jayde and could have information on his death. He could also be a suspect himself.

I took the photo up to the shop clerk and asked if he could reprint the photo with an enlargement of the two faces in the photo. The guy behind the counter recognized me from previous investigation business that I had had with him so he had no problems doing that for me while I waited.

Trying to identify this mysterious man might be more difficult. If anyone could help me it was Chief Purser Gardner. The Purser usually meets or comes in contact with everyone on the ship at some time or another.

"Brad, I've got a lead that I want to check out with the Purser. I'm sure he's on duty still this evening. How about I meet up with you later?"

Brad seemed to be getting tired. "Sounds fine to me. I've seen just about all I care to anyway here. I'll meet you at the disco later."

Thankfully, Purser Gardner was in his office along with another crew member.

"Kyle, do you recognize this passenger? The one is Jayde, but not sure who he is with."

Purser Gardner took the picture from me and looked closely at the subjects. "He looks really familiar. I know I've waited on him for some services."

"Think about it. It's really important."

"Now I recall. He cashed a check here just a few days ago. Let me call it up on the computer. We scan their driver's license so I can get a name for you. Hold on."

I was thrilled to be getting this information and wanted to talk to this guy first thing in the morning.

"Here you go …his name is Colton Anders. His license indicates he's from Chicago."

"Can I get a copy of that, his license?"

"Sure, hold on a second."

I recalled Bill and Jayde saying they were from Chicago that first night we met them on the ship in the dining room. I felt I was finally on to something.

 ∾

It was early morning the last day at sea. I had let Brad know what I was on to and at eight o'clock I was on the bridge talking with the Captain. I needed to check out this guy Colton. The Captain allowed me to make a ship-to-shore call to my office.

"Good morning, Balboa Investigators. How may I direct your call?"

"Morning, Jenn. It's Tony."

Jenn was excited to hear from me I could tell. "Oh, Mr. Felice, where are you? Are you all right? We saw the news about the ship fire. Are you okay?" I noticed shortly after my promotion to CEO that Jenn had started addressing me as Mr. Felice instead of Tony, obviously recognizing that I am now her boss.

"Thanks, Jenn. We're fine. I need your help however."

"Sure, what do you need, Mr. Felice?"

"I need you to run a criminal background check for me."

I gave her Colton's driver's license number and she ran a check while I waited on the phone. The results were just as I suspected. Colton had a police record, everything from drunk in public to assault and battery. One of his convictions was for embezzlement. It was looking like this was the kind of guy who might have some connection to Jayde's murder. But how were they connected?

I asked the Captain to have a couple of security guards escort Colton to the bridge so I could talk to him.

"Morning, Mr. Anders. Come in. Have a seat." The Captain was trying to make Colton feel comfortable and relaxed but he seemed nervous to me.

"So what's this about? Why am I here?" Colton seemed puzzled.

"I'm Tony Felice, a Private Investigator. Do you recognize this man?" I showed him a picture of Jayde.

"Sure, that's the guy that was in the ship's bulletin, the one that was found dead."

"Right! And how well did you know this guy?"

"I didn't know him. I just seen him on the ship a few times."

"Were you having an affair with him or was it just a fling?"

"I told you, I never knew Jayde. His picture is familiar to me. That's all."

"I never told you his name, Colton. So you knew him as Jayde? This picture indicates to me that you knew each other quite well. Care to explain?" I showed Colton the picture of the two of them making out. He looked shocked.

"Well, yeah, we did make out one time, but that was

all. I could hardly say I knew him."

This scenario actually fit with Jayde's MO and could have been believable if it were not for the other information I had on Colton's background.

I decided to go out on a limb here and try something that might get him to talk. "All right, Colton, I'm going to level with you. We have a witness who saw you that night at the pool, coming from the service closet the night Jayde was murdered. Why don't you tell us about it? What happened?"

"No one was there. ...No one saw me. ...Everyone had gone out on deck. It was an accident. ...I didn't mean for it to happen."

That was pretty much of a confession. I felt a tingle down my spine knowing I was finally on the edge of putting all the puzzle pieces together. I sat back in my chair and took a long breath before proceeding.

"So how did it happen, Colton? What led you to kill Jayde?"

Colton sighed and stared off, away from our conversation. He seemed to be surrendering to the inevitable, and ready to talk.

"Go ahead, Colton, start from the beginning. How did you know Jayde?"

Colton just shook his head as he rested it in his hands. After a brief silence he began, "I didn't intend for it to happen. ...I met Jayde probably four or five months ago at the bath house back home. It started out just being an anonymous sexual thing but each time we met there, we hooked up. We eventually started arranging to meet at my house and once in a while at his. I never met Bill but had seen pictures of him."

"So you were having an affair with Jayde behind Bill's back?"

"It was more than an affair. It started out that way but we fell in love somewhere along the way. Jayde wanted to leave Bill but he liked the security that Bill offered him. Jayde never wanted to work and had no money of his own. He was a user and I knew that, but I loved him."

"Did Jayde continue to be promiscuous even after the two of you became romantically involved?" I knew perfectly well the answer to that question.

Colton answered softly, "He did, yes."

"And how did that make you feel?"

Colton took a deep breath. "At first I was okay with it but it got to be old with me and I wanted Jayde to love me and only me. His sexual escapades bothered me but I knew he would change over time if only he could just leave Bill and become dependent on me instead."

"So Colton, was this trip just to be closer to Jayde? Is that what prompted it?"

Colton continued, "Jayde kept telling me he had to break up with Bill but he didn't like breaking up with his money. So just about a month before the cruise, Jayde told me he and Bill had recently taken out large life insurance policies on each other, and that he planned to kill Bill while on the cruise. He said accidents happen on cruise ships all the time. At first I was shocked and thought his plan was pretty absurd. But then I thought it just might work and then Jayde and I could live a happy life together with the money from the life insurance."

"So did you conspire with Jayde at this point?"

"Jayde was too scatter-brained to pull this off without my help. I told him I'd help but I had to go on the cruise and we'd have to remain strangers on the ship to avoid suspicion. He was fine with that and actually excited with the thought of me going with them. There was a last minute cancellation so I was able to get a reservation on the cruise and the plan was set in motion. Jayde planned to get Bill drunk one evening and push him overboard. I could help him and it wouldn't be until the next day before Bill would be reported missing."

"Okay, Colton, let's cut to the chase now. Tell us how and why you murdered Jayde."

Colton took a deep breath and a sip from the bottle of water the Captain had brought him earlier. He began to tell the story of the last few minutes of Jayde's life and the role he played in his death.

16

Mystery Solved

Colton began, "It was the night of the disaster at sea. Jayde and I had made plans to meet up at the indoor pool but then he showed up with Bill. I had to keep my distance and act like a stranger. I was irritated with this right away. I'd hoped for a little time alone with Jayde that night."

"So then at some point did you connect with him?"

"We started talking like two guys meeting for the first time. There were other guys there as well and we all laughed and joked in the pool. Then we ended up in the spa, without our swim suits and just sort of played around."

I asked, "Was Jayde horsing around too?"

"He was out of control. I'd never seen him like this and I was getting more furious with his behavior by the minute. He was enjoying the attention.

"At one point he left the spa and slipped behind a door with one of the crew members. I wanted to follow him but I didn't. Then just before the emergency alarm,

I noticed Bill had slipped behind that door as well, so I was really curious. Once the alarm went off, everyone started to scramble for their suits and head out to their lifeboat stations. I decided to duck behind that door and see what was going on."

"And so what did you find once you were there?" I asked.

"I stayed in the shadows but I watched Bill and Jayde argue and struggle for a while.

"Realizing that Jayde and Bill were getting very physical I was concerned that something might happen to Jayed ...or to Bill too for that matter. I knew I had to get out of there, however, because I kept hearing the alarm blasting away and it was obvious this was something serious. I returned to the pool, grabbed my towel and started to head out to the deck to my lifeboat station. But as I started to leave, I became concerned that Jayde needed to get out of there too and wondered if he needed my help. I decided to go back and check on him."

"Did you see Bill when you went back? Was he still there?"

"No, no one was there except Jayde who seemed to be roughed up. He was standing by the spa, trying to put his suit on. ...If there was someone else there, I never saw them."

"Did you approach Jayde then? And what'd you say to him?"

"My disgust and jealousy came over me once again.

I called him…" He started to sob again. "I called him a fucking whore -- but I regretted that as soon as I said it."

"So did that start a fight between you two?"

"He was really upset over what I'd said, and he turned around and pushed me away. I pushed back and he fell into the spa hitting his head. I jumped into the spa to drag him out and see if he was all right. Once I got hold of him, he came to and started to fight me. He was screaming at me and not making a lot of sense. He said something about me thinking I was better than he was. He took a swing at me and nailed me in the mouth."

"Then what happened, Colton?"

"I hit him back with my fist and he was stunned. As soon as I hit him, I was overcome by my anger with him and his behavior. That's when I did it. I lost my temper completely, and I choked him, holding him under the water until his body quit struggling. I pulled back almost immediately but realized it was too late – he was gone.

"I was shocked when I saw what I'd done, and I was plenty scared. I knew that Bill and Jayde had been seen together earlier in that service closet so I decided to move Jayde into the closet and dump his body into the water tube. I knew he'd be found eventually.

"I figured Bill would be implicated in the murder. Just before lowering Jayde's body into the water, I noticed on the floor the gold pendant I'd seen Bill wearing and tossed it into the water tube as well, giving more reason to suspect Bill of Jayde's death."

"Then what happened?"

"I left, going to my lifeboat station. Everything was so fucked up now. It wasn't supposed to happen this way. I was scared and I didn't even realize anyone had seen me in the pool area when all this happened. I figured I could just pretend like this didn't happen and maybe Bill would be considered the obvious murderer."

"Actually, Colton, there was no witness who saw you, but that little lie accomplished what I wanted. You are under arrest now and will be handcuffed in your room with a guard tending to you until we get back to the pier in San Diego. At that time you'll be turned over to the police to stand trial for Jayde's murder."

I was very pleased to have solved this murder -- and just in time before returning to San Diego. The Captain was grateful and delighted and, on behalf of the cruise line, congratulated me, letting me know that they were very happy to have this all settled. He said that by solving the crime before reaching port, the cruise line could hopefully move on without any major negative publicity.

The Captain also informed me he would have a corporate check for my services before I left the ship. I made sure their bill was not conservative after the challenges

I'd faced. And since our cruise had been interrupted with a near catastrophic incident and a long, frightening night without food, combined with the fear of a lifeboat evacuation, I felt my compensation was well deserved.

I was able to spend the rest of the day relaxing without any further stress and distraction of an investigation and it felt good. I wanted to make the most of what little time I had left with Brad and the other guys on the ship before debarkation the following morning.

17

Happy Endings

We spent part of the remainder of the day relaxing by the pool and having drinks while listening to the steel pan reggae music. It seemed that things were all back to normal with the ship, even after a fire disaster at sea and a murder aboard. How quickly we forget. Brad and I'd decided to accept the offer of a free future cruise as our adjustment for the inconvenience of the fire and cancelled cruise itinerary.

That evening we were required to put our luggage in the hallway to be removed in preparation for debarkation. In the morning we woke up docked at the pier in San Diego. We had breakfast with the guys one last time.

After breakfast, the passengers were told to wait in one of the auditoriums, lounge areas or on the upper deck around the pool until Customs cleared our ship for us to disembark. Brad was adamant that we should all go to the upper deck around the pool.

I was feeling down knowing that this cruise was over and we were headed back to the routine of everyday life. I really didn't care where we waited to be called to leave the ship. It was a beautiful clear morning on the coast of San Diego but that still didn't make the fact that the cruise was over any easier on me. I was so looking forward to the trek through the locks of the Panama, and disappointed now to be home without having done that. Brad and I would likely re-schedule a Panama crossing cruise in the future for our compensation for this cruise cancelation.

"Let's go over to the other side, okay guys?" Brad was trying to organize the six of us.

"Sure, Brad. We can see the people getting off the ship on that side too." John agreed.

"Over there near the pool bar, near the Jumbotron TV." Brad seemed very diligent in organizing us, but I could feel myself becoming more melancholy with time.

We found a spot on the upper pool deck near the Jumbotron TV as Brad had requested and prepared to sit back and wait for maybe a couple of hours or more. I was thinking of all that I had to do once I got back to the office. My mind was drifting away from the conversation, not wanting to dwell on the fact this cruise was over.

The other passengers were pretty solemn as well, realizing they were all headed home. I could hear the faint sound of an engine in the distance. As it got louder, I realized it was the sound of an airplane. We all looked to the sky to see a bi-plane approaching the ship, pulling a banner. I figured it was likely some advertisement, but like all of us, I was curious to try and see what it said as it got closer.

Finally it was close enough to read. The guys on the upper deck all began to cheer and then I realized what I was seeing. The banner read, 'MARRY ME TONY? LUV U, BRAD'. I was speechless and my heart was nearly beating out of my chest. And then I noticed the two of us in all our splendor, featured on the Jumbotron TV for everyone to see. What happened next brought me to tears. Brad got down on one knee and proposed, asking me to marry him. Of course I said yes and the guys on the deck went crazy with cheers, whistles and applause. I threw myself into his arms and we kissed for what seemed to be an eternity. The Jumbotron caught every minute of our elation to be shared with the crowd. It was for me a fairy tale ending to our cruise that I never would have predicted and will never forget.

❧

After returning to work I found myself immersed in learning the operations of Balboa Private Investigators. There was a lot I still needed to learn.

I'd turned over the DNA evidence I gathered on the cruise to the police. Their investigation determined that under Jayde's fingernails was DNA from both Bill and Colton. The Krugerrand registration was identified as belonging to Bill, but with Colton's confession, there was no question as to who killed Jayde.

Much later, I learned something ironic about the life insurance policy that Jayde insisted he and Bill purchase on each other before the cruise. The policy on Jayde had paid off the million dollars, but not to Bill. Taking into account his age and his financial stability, Bill had removed himself as beneficiary on Jayde's policy, and substituted the names of his four grandchildren. Sweet irony – Bill's family became wealthy after Jayde's death, instead of Jayde being in that position after he planned for Bill's death.

Brad and I started making plans for our wedding even though the date we'd chosen was at least nine months away. We knew we wanted to get married in Palm Springs, with a good friend of ours, Michael Green from Triangle Inn officiating. Other than that, we had no definite plans and didn't want all the decision making getting in the way of our relationship as sometimes happens.

We had decided to take a honeymoon trip using our complementary cruise to finally make the trek through the locks of the Panama. Our friend Robb at ExtaSea Cruises was already working on that for us. We were taking things slowly and would be happy to have a small ceremony with just the two of us and our witness. Life was getting back to normal for the both of us but I was looking forward to the day, soon, when I could introduce Brad as my husband.

"…Still waters run deep."

Acknowledgements

I would like to thank all my family and friends who supported me in the creation of this, the third book in the Tony Felice mystery series. A special thank you to Sonya Cox for all the many hours spent editing my writing and making me look good.

And . . . I'm sorry for having cursed my high school English teacher, Barbara Cannon. Thanks for teaching me some useful skills in life. Believe me, I appreciate you now.

And . . . for making the first impression of my book so appealing and the formatting so easily readable, thank you to Mark Anderson of AquaZebra.com.

And . . . a special thank you to Palm Springs Koffi, south end, for keeping my coffee cup full and putting up with me for all the hours spent writing this book at the coffee shop.

And . . . thanks also to Raphael and Charlotte for the artistic inspiration I gleaned from their French café, L'Atelier, and for allowing me so many hours hanging out while allowing my creativity to flourish.

And . . . I appreciate my sister-in-law, Cleusa de Magalhaes, and her Brazilian Portuguese translations.

And lastly, I can't forget to thank Lulu Palm Springs restaurant for giving me the inspiration for the water tube described in my book based on the water feature in front of their restaurant.

Did you enjoy reading about
Tony's adventure?
Want to read more?
Look for

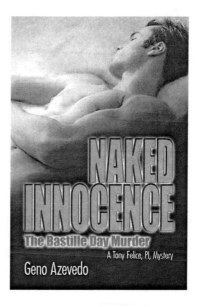

Book 1   **Book 2**

Available on Amazon

www.TonyFeliceMystery.com